The Red Scarf

The Red Scarf

Richard Mason

August House Publishers, Inc.
ATLANTA

Published 2007
by August House Publishers, Inc.
3500 Piedmont Road NE, Suite 310
Atlanta, Georgia 30305
404-442-4420
http://www.augusthouse.com

Book design by H. K. Stewart

Manufactured in the United States
10 9 8 7 6 5 4 3 2 1

LIBRARY OF CONGRESS CATALOGING-IN-PUBLICATION DATA

Mason, Richard Harper.
The red scarf / Richard Mason.
p. cm.
Summary: In the winter of 1944, eleven-year-old Richard has adventures
living on a small farm in Arkansas.
ISBN 978-0-87483-850-3 (hardcover : alk. paper)
[1. Country life--Arkansas--Fiction. 2. Friendship--Fiction. 3. Schools--Fiction.
4. Arkansas--History--1933-1945--Fiction.] I. Title.

PZ7.M42315Re 2007
[Fic]--dc22
2007027480

The paper used in this publication meets the minimum requirements of the
American National Standards for Information Sciences—Permanence of Paper
for Printed Library Materials, ANSI. 48–1984.

To Vertis...

who will always be my first reader

Acknowledgments

I heard Studs Turkle, who was being interviewed by Andy Rooney, give a bit of advice to new writers, "Write remembrances." That's what I've tried to do as I sat at the word processor and thought back to a time when young Southern boys went barefooted all summer and their entertainment was their imagination.

There is something about growing up in the rural South that produces a different type of person than the rest of the country. Maybe it's the struggle to overcome a myriad of disadvantages that are endemic to the South, or possibly it's the strong women who instill in their sons and daughters determination and grit to persevere. My mother was one of those women, who never let poverty, an alcoholic husband, or lack of an education hold her back. She held our family together when by all odds it should have disintegrated.

Remembering those times and writing about them has given me a great deal of pleasure, but more than that I hope it will give you, the reader, a better understanding of the simple pleasures and sometimes frightening experiences that were part of every country boy's life in the late 1940s. The outlandish pranks, adventures, and dangers these young Southern boys were involved in are actual real-life experiences selected from the early childhoods of rural farm boys in the South.

I would like to thank my many friends who have encouraged me to work and get my novels published, and I especially want to thank August House for taking a chance on a new writer and publishing *The Red Scarf.*

Every writer understands that a novel is a complex relationship that evolves over months and sometimes years as an author's imagination ebbs and flows, churning out chapter after chapter. But it's more than that. The input, comments, and yes, even the criticisms all go into making the final manuscript. I've had a lot of encouragement from readers who have made those long rewrites seem worthwhile, and I'd like to give special thanks to that group of women who have read, commented, and enjoyed my novels: Candi Nolan, Diane Alderson, Jannis Echols, and of course, my first reader, Vertis, my wonderful wife.

In every process, whether it's writing a novel or doing anything else of value that can be improved with input from other skilled individuals, there is always someone whose tireless dedication stands out above all others. That person is Bettie Anne Mahony, English professor at South Arkansas Community College. Without Bettie Anne's red pencil and her sidebar comments my works would be severely lacking. A special thanks to Bettie Anne for all those hours when she pored over page after page of my work.

1

The Nail

Monday, January 1st, 1945

Ohoooo! Dang! Dang! For gosh sakes, I thought I was gonna freeze to death this morning walking that sorry paper route! My shoes are wet from all that leftover melting snow, and as skinny as I am that cold north wind just blows right through me. I'm standing here in front of our fireplace shaking like a leaf. Shoot, I guess I'd better take off these cold wet shoes, or I'm never gonna dry out and get warm. My fingers are so numb I can't hardly undo these shoelaces, but—ahaa, now they're coming off, and I'm sitting them shoes down in front of the fire to dry them out. Heck, I'd better take off these wet socks too.—Whew! Dang, this fire feels good! Now they're off, and I'm gonna put them close to the fire.

Hey, look at my cold white feet. Don't they look funny? White, white, white, of course, except for them two pink scars, and shoot, look at them long scabs running down my leg. Well, that ain't all; just looky at them two little red places that look like holes. Heck, when I just think about everything that happened to me, I guess I'm lucky to be here at all. Course, it seems like that kinda stuff always happens to me, and heck, one of these days I'm gonna get ahold of something I can't turn loose of, and I'll be a goner—dead as a fence post—just laid out cold as a sack of hammers.

Well, I guess you want to hear about the whole dang mess, don't you? Huh? Every little thing? Well,—let's see—; first off, this here pink scar on the top of my foot and the other one on the bottom happened at the end of summer and these pink scratches with the scabs on the side of my leg happened just a couple of weeks ago. Them two red looking holes was caused by something that happened right before Christmas, and none of them have got nothing to do with each other. Can you believe that? Well, it's true, cross my heart, and it still gives me the willies, every time I think about it.

Okay; first let me tell you how I got them two pink scars, the one on top and the one on the bottom of my foot. They's the ones that hurt the most. Listen, I can't even come close to telling you how much my foot hurt.

I guess it was sometime right after Labor Day, and I was just out roaming around in the woods looking for chinkapin trees, when I happened to walk by Uncle Hugh's cabin. Me and John Clayton, my best friend, call this old colored man Uncle Hugh. Course he ain't my uncle and I don't really know why we call him uncle, it just seems like that's what we ought to call him. Anyway he's old—heck—I mean really, really old, and he ain't been doing real well. We were worried about him since last summer cause he was having trouble walking in to town. After he just walks back from the spring where he gets his water, he's breathing so hard he has to sit down. I sure ain't no doctor, but heck, it don't take no doctor to tell Uncle Hugh's in real bad shape.

Well, we know Uncle Hugh real good, cause a couple of years ago me and John Clayton was a-wandering through the woods playing Tarzan, and we got lost as a couple of gooses. Thank the good Lord, we just happened to stumble upon Uncle Hugh's little cabin, and Uncle Hugh walked back to town with us. We've been coming by to visit him ever since. Gosh, he can tell great stories about the olden days, and he's one of our bestest friends. Course, I get real sad when I talk about Uncle Hugh cause of what happened at Christmas, but shoot, that ain't got nothing to do with these scars and scratches. I'll tell you about them after I tell you what happened at Uncle Hugh's cabin that day. Ohoooo, dang, just thinking about it makes a shiver run down my spine.

That Saturday afternoon I decided I'd stop by and visit with Uncle Hugh for a few minutes, so I ran up on his porch and yelled, "Uncle Hugh! Uncle Hugh!" and then I took off like a scalded dog across the porch and went a-flying off the side. Shoot, I was gonna fool old Uncle Hugh and hide under his porch and make him wonder where I was. Boy, I can remember that jump just like it was yesterday. I sailed off the porch, which was about four feet off the ground, and I remember looking down just before I hit, and I saw a bunch of boards on the ground. Heck, I thought, just some boards, that ain't gonna make no difference, and I blambed down right on top of one big long plank.

Oh, my God in heaven above! I ain't never felt nothing in my whole born days like that. Something had stuck in my bare left foot, and I knew dang well it weren't no little sticker. Well, I fell over screaming my head off, and then I realized my foot was stuck to the board. In a hundred million years you'd never believe what I saw when I looked down. I almost fainted. I'd jumped off the porch and landed smack dab on a stuck-up nail that was a-sticking in the board, and I just hadn't stuck a nail in my foot; oh no, the nail had gone plum through my foot and was sticking out the top of my foot. You wouldn't believe how bad that hurt.

I was screaming, crying, and yelling as I tried to pull the nail out of my foot, but it was hurting so much I couldn't. I fell over on the ground moaning, trying to keep the nail still where it wouldn't hurt so much, when I heard Uncle Hugh calling, "Richard! Richard! What wrong?" In just a little bit he came down the steps and hurried over to where I was lying. He took one look at me and said, "Oh, my good Lord! Oh, my Lord. We gotta get that nail outta yo foot, Richard."

"Don't touch it, Uncle Hugh! It hurts a whole bunch more when the nail moves!" I'm not a-kidding you, before I'd pull that nail back through my foot, I'd just rather somebody cold-cock me and knock me out like a light.

"Richard, we gotta pull that nail outta yo foot. There ain't no way to get you to town like that." Course I tried to stop him, but he just kept on. Uncle Hugh pulled a rope out of his pocket and handed it to me. "Now Richard, just bite down on this rope and close yo eyes."

"No! No! Don't touch it!" I was begging, yelling, and crying, but finally I took the thick rope and bit down on it, and then Uncle Hugh took my foot and yanked that nail right back through my foot. Oh my good Lord in heaven above, I thought it really hurt when the nail went through my foot, but when Uncle Hugh pulled that nail back out of my foot, it hurt so much I couldn't even yell. Then, when I finally got my breath, I let out a blood-curdling scream you could've heard a mile away. Well, Uncle Hugh was right; it did feel a little better after a few minutes, and I tried to stand up, but when I put any weight down on it, I'd just fall over cause it hurt so much.

Uncle Hugh looked at me and bent over.

"Richard, I'm gonna pick you up and carry you into the cabin and doctor yo foot."

Uncle Hugh scooped me up and carried me into his cabin, laid me out on his bed, and in a few minutes he came back with a bandage and some salve and leaves.

"Richard, I'm gonna put this here poultice on both sides of that nail hole and bandage it up real good. Then we'll see 'bout gettin' you home."

"What's in the poultice, Uncle Hugh?"

"Some poke sallet leaves, a little ground-up cayenne pepper, some fatback, and a dab of bacon drippings. It'll draw out the poison that the nail left in yo foot."

Well, I was hurting so much that I didn't care what Uncle Hugh put on my foot, but I was wondering how in the world I was gonna get home. There weren't no way on God's green earth I could walk. It didn't take long for Uncle Hugh to put the bandage and poultice on my foot, and in a few minutes my foot did feel a little better. It was getting kinda late in the day, and I knew I needed to be heading home. I was sitting on the edge of the bed, and I tried to stand up and put some weight on my hurt foot, but as soon as it touched the floor—oh, you wouldn't believe how it hurt. I grabbed the bed and quit trying to stand up.

"What am I gonna do, Uncle Hugh? I can't walk home on this foot!"

"Richard, there ain't but one way to get you home. I's gotta carry you."

"Oh, Uncle Hugh; it's too far, you can't carry me all the way to my house, it's almost a mile through the woods."

"I done been thinkin' 'bout it, Richard, and they ain't no other way. So you just relax, and we'll get started."

Before I could say another word, Uncle Hugh picked me up and started walking out the cabin door and down the steps. I'm not a very big kid, but I was almost twelve years old and weighed sixty-five pounds. I didn't think Uncle Hugh could carry me all the way to my house, and if he tried, I was sure he'd just fall over or drop dead.

"Uncle Hugh, put me down. My foot feels a lot better, and I can walk." Well, even though my foot hurt like nothing I've ever felt, I wasn't gonna let an old colored man, who was older than God, carry me a mile in his arms. But as soon as I put my foot down I knew I couldn't walk. I tried to hop on one leg, but heck, hopping along on one foot is okay for a little bit; then you get so tired you fall over, and after I did that a couple of times and stepped down on my sore foot, I quit trying to hop and Uncle Hugh picked me up. It took Uncle Hugh almost an hour to carry me home, and by the time we were about halfway there he was having to stop every twenty yards to rest. He was just gasping for breath and his legs were shaking something terrible. I was sure he was gonna fall over and not be able to get back up, and I was gonna be stranded out in the woods, and I'd hafta crawl home, or we'd just lie there and holler for someone to come help us. But Uncle Hugh just wouldn't give up, and finally we came up out of the creek bottom, and I could see my house right down the road.

It was after six o'clock when Uncle Hugh made it to my front gate, and I started screaming for Momma and Daddy. Momma came running out of the house with Daddy right behind her. She was a-yelling. "Richard! Richard! What happened? Are you all right?"

"Miss Sue, Richard, he done stepped on a nail," said Uncle Hugh, who was so out of breath he could barely speak.

"Oh, my God, Richard! If it not one thing it's another! You're not gonna see your twelfth birthday if you don't quit getting hurt."

Daddy came up and took me out of Uncle Hugh's arms, and Uncle Hugh stumbled over and sat on our porch steps.

"Mister Jack—I done cleaned up the nail hole—and put a good poultice on it.—He's gonna be all right."

"Hugh, how far did you carry Richard?"

"All the way from my house, Mister Jack—and I gotta rest a little bit before I walks back."

"Hugh, you just sit right there and rest, and as soon as I take care of Richard, I'll give you a ride back."

Daddy sat me down on the porch steps, and Momma took off the bandage and looked at where the nail had gone through my foot. She shook her head and then put the bandage back around my foot.

"My grandmother used to put a poultice on any puncture wound, and I think since Hugh cleaned up the wound, I'll just leave it be," Mother said. "Well, I guess that tetanus shot you got a couple of weeks ago when you cut your hand on that rusty piece of tin will still be good."

Daddy got Uncle Hugh in the car and drove him back to his house, and Momma helped me into the house where I plopped up on the couch. Sure enough, Uncle Hugh's poultice pulled the poison out of where the nail stuck me, and in a few days I was hobbling around. Heck, in a week, I was almost good as new.

2

Sniffer Attacks a Chicken-Killing Coon

Monday, January 1st, 1945

Course I'll never forget about old Uncle Hugh carrying me back through the woods all the way to my house, and after a couple of weeks, when my foot healed, me and John Clayton started going by Uncle Hugh's cabin a whole lot more cause we could tell he was having trouble walking, but I'll get to that part of the story in a little bit.

But right now it's New Year's Day, and I'm sitting in front of our fireplace trying to thaw out after delivering those sorry papers and doing my chores. Dang, this has been the most God-awful winter I've ever known, and we've still got a bunch to go. Heck, sitting here in front of the fireplace, listening to the wood crackle and staring at them burning logs, I can't keep from thinking about everything that happened around Christmas, and heck, it weren't just around Christmas; the dang stuff started way before that, right after Thanksgiving.

My gosh, after a summer and fall where I got into stuff that almost got me killed, I'd dang sure figured Christmas would be real quiet. Shoot, I was real wrong about that, but you know, even after all that stuff happened, it was still my best Christmas ever. Whew; just thinking back on everything that went on after Thanksgiving makes me tired. Course, I guess you want to hear every little old thing about them scratches on my leg and them red-hole-looking things; so here goes.

Friday, November 24th, 1944

The stuff all started the day after Thanksgiving, real early that Friday morning. Heck, it seems like it was just yesterday. The first thing I remember, even before I got out of bed, was the sound of a cold north wind rattling the tin roof on our little old white-frame farm house. I'd kicked off my quilt sometime during the night before the cold front roared in, and I was freezing to death. Let me tell you one thing right now; I'm one skinny boy, and I can't stand cold weather. I'd just woke up, and I was trying to pull the quilt back over my head, when that dang alarm clock went off.

"Uh; uh, dang, oh, not five o'clock already," I mumbled as I slapped it to stop the racket.

I sat up in bed, rubbing the sleep out of my eyes, and stepped out on the cold, wooden floor, shivering as I grabbed for my jeans and sweatshirt. Then I heard something.

Hoooooooooo, hooooooo, hooooo, hooooo. It was old Sniffer.

What in the world is Sniffer howling about? I thought. Sniffer, my skinny old mixed-breed hound was howling like a dog gone crazy somewhere out in the back yard. I yanked on my jeans, pulled my sweatshirt over my head, and ran barefoot out our back door.

"Good Lord, Sniffer! What's got into you? Hush! You're gonna wake up Momma and Daddy." Sniffer didn't pay me no mind. He was a-running up and down beside the dark, fenced-in chicken yard wailing a long hound howl, pawing at the fence like he was after something. It was so dark I could barely see the chicken house, but old Sniffer could sure enough smell something.

"What is it, Sniffer? Whata you smell? Is somethin' in the chicken house?" I hollered.

Sniffer just bawled out another bunch of howls loud enough to wake the dead, and I ran over to the gate.

"Here, Sniffer, come on; go git 'em! Sic 'em! Sic 'em! Eyaaaaa! Go git 'em, Sniffer!" I opened the gate to the chicken yard and clapped my hands as I sicced him after whatever was in the chicken house.

"Eeeee! Yhaaaa! Git 'em, Sniffer! Get that dang coon! Yeah! I'll just bet 'nother one of them dang coons is up from the swamp tryin' to catch a chicken!" Sniffer dashed into the dark chicken yard, heading straight for the chicken house, where the chickens were a-squawking like nothing you've ever heard.

"Get 'em, Sniffer! Get 'em! Eeeeeee! Yhaaaaa!"

By gollee, Sniffer was all worked up, and he ran up the plank into the chicken house and through the little door like a flash, and Holy Cow, a roar went up like nothing you've ever heard, I mean in your whole life, as Sniffer clomped down on that coon.

"Eeeeeee! Yahaaaaa! Git 'em! Git 'em! Git that dang coon, Sniffer!" I screamed. I thought about going in the chicken house and helping Sniffer, but I'd decided I wasn't about to get in no coon–dog fight, cause the last time I did, Sniffer bit the fire out of me, thinking I was the coon.

Well, Sniffer stopped howling when he bit down on the coon, but not for long. Soon I heard another sound, something like a coon going crazy and a hound a-hurting.

"Dang! What in the heck is goin' on?" I peered through the chicken-wire fence and tried to see what was happening, but I couldn't see a dang thing but a bunch of out-of-their-mind chickens running round the yard cackling to beat sixty.

My gosh, I tell you, chickens was a-flooding out of the little door of the chicken house running for their lives, cackling up a storm, and you could hear old Sniffer and the coon bouncing off the walls. Good Lord, they was a-screeching and a-howling like crazy. It weren't but a few seconds when I heard Sniffer yelping like he was getting whipped, and it sounded like the coon was winning the fight.

"What? What?—Git 'em! Git 'em; Sniffer! Eyeeeee! Yahaaaaa!" I hooped and hollered, trying to encourage old Sniffer.

Shoot, there ain't a coon in these parts that can whip old Sniffer, I thought, but I'll be danged, in another few seconds—after the yelping and growling and snarling just went clean out of sight—bursting out of the chicken house came a whipped-up and bloodied old

Sniffer with his head down and his tail between his legs. Then there was just a blur as the biggest dang coon I've ever seen in my whole blessed entire life done come a-running out of that chicken house, jumped the little wire fence, and skedaddled. It was so dark I could barely see the coon as it headed out across our garden.

"Well, I'll be a son-of-a-gun; the dang big coon whipped Sniffer," I said, shaking my head.

I walked back to the house, where old Sniffer was sitting by the back porch steps, whining like some old whipped-up-on dog.

"You sorry worthless hound! Let a dang old coon whip you? I can't believe it! Good Lord in heaven above, what in the heck is wrong with you?" I talk to Sniffer a lot, and even if he is a dog, I think he can understand me.

Well, Sniffer hung his head like a sorry whipped-up-on dog would do as he rubbed his chewed-up ear against the porch steps. *Heck,* I thought, *that dog can usually take out a coon or possum with one quick bite. This musta been a big 'un.* I reached down and patted Sniffer as I walked back toward the house to get my flashlight and put on some shoes. Dang, my feet were frozen.

Sniffer let out another howl just for good measure and trotted back to the chicken yard fence where he growled and pawed the dirt.

"Ha, you better be glad that dang coon's long gone, Sniffer," I hollered at him as I went back in the house. Sniffer raised his head and gave out the longest howl—oh you wouldn't believe how that dog was hopping round. I laughed so hard.

Well, that's good old Sniffer. He's my worthless, and I mean worthless, old hound dog and though he let a big old coon whip him, I can count on him, and he never leaves my side unless I'm in school. Every day when I get home he's waiting for me, welcoming me with one after another of those long hound howls that you can hear all the way across our little forty-acre farm. Course Sniffer always wants to go down into Flat Creek Swamp hunting, and that's what we do most afternoons. But, heck, that's all we do is hunt. Sniffer lives up to his name every time we're in the woods. He howls, and he sniffs and sniffs as he howls to beat sixty, but that's it. He's just a sniffer. Heck, didn't I tell you he was worthless? Oh, sometimes he'll run across a sorry old possum, but most of the time it's just an afternoon of howling and sniffing when we're hunting.

I live way down in south Arkansas right on the edge of big Flat Creek Swamp, and I've had Sniffer for a couple of months now. One Friday afternoon last fall, Pop Davis, an old river rat who lives down near Moro Bay on the Ouachita River, drove up in his old pickup with Sniffer riding in the back. He hollered at me and asked if I wanted a good hunting dog. Course I did, and Daddy let me have him. Pop said he was getting too old to hunt, but Daddy told me later that Pop's moonshine still was keeping him busy and he was sampling his moonshine all the time. I think that had something to do with his not hunting cause he had a wild bloodshot look in his eyes, and when he drove off in that old truck he was going back and forth all across the road.

I guess I shouldn't call Sniffer worthless cause Sniffer's really a dang good dog, and he's the best friend an eleven-year-old boy could have, but this is the first time I've seen a coon get the best of old Sniffer. Course he ain't perfect; he's an egg-sucking hound. When we first got Sniffer, he had the run of the farm, but one afternoon I noticed eggs were missing, and later that day I spotted Sniffer walking out of the chicken-yard carrying an egg in his mouth. He went over by the barn and bit down on one end and sucked the inside out.

"Dang you, Sniffer!" I yelled, and I kicked eggshells all over the place. Daddy had a conniption fit when he found out and was gonna shoot Sniffer, but I talked him out of it and helped him build a fence around the chicken yard. That's why the chicken yard has a fence and gate, and I can't put Sniffer in the chicken house to run off the big old coon that's after the chickens.

We're the Mason family, and we live on a little forty-acre farm in south Arkansas. I'm Richard, my momma's Sue, and my daddy's Jack.

I'm in the sixth grade, the town paperboy, and I'm a pretty tall boy for my age, but I'm kinda thin; shoot, I'm not just kinda thin,

I'm downright skinny, and dang; cold weather turns me into an icicle. Everybody says I look a whole lot like my momma, and maybe I do. We both have coal black hair, and she's as skinny as I am.

Daddy works for McMillan Refinery, and I guess he's got a pretty good job, cause when he tried to enlist in the army after the dang Japs bombed us, they froze him on his job. Said he could do more to win the war by working at the refinery.

Boy, about a year ago, me and Daddy were sitting around listening to Walter Winchell, the famous newscaster, and Daddy was telling me how bad the war was. Heck, today, a year later, we've almost whipped them sorry Germans, and Daddy said once we get through with them, the Japs has had it.

It's not long 'til Christmas, and things are in one heck of a mess at our house cause of my daddy's drinking. Shoot, it seems like everything's always in a mess around our house. Right before Thanksgiving, Daddy came in drunk, and the whole family got into a big fight. The fight got so bad that I got knocked out accidentally, and Daddy was so upset he promised never to drink again, but that didn't last a week. He's got a good job at the refinery, but his weekend beer drinking—buying beer for all his sorry friends and loaning them money—keeps our family broke.

Momma's about all that holds our family together. She's great. Early every morning she'll be out in the barn milking old Jersey, our milk cow, and that afternoon when I come in from school, she'll be sewing on some high-fashion dress. Momma has real white skin, dark brown eyes and long black hair which curls down around her face. Daddy's always grumbling about men in town flirting with her, so I guess she's real pretty.

As far as I'm concerned, things are set around our house. I get up at five o'clock, go run my dang paper route, get on back home, feed the chickens and mules, eat breakfast, and walk to school. I've got two pair of jeans for school and a pair of dress pants for church. I've grown about two inches since Momma bought them last year, so the bottoms of the trousers hit right above my ankles, and the cuffs on my two long-sleeve shirts fit about the same. But, heck, that's the way most of my friends dress. Sometimes I wear a pair of overalls with straps that clip in the front and have buttons along the side, and last year Momma bought me a heavy jacket that I wear almost every day after it gets cold.

Christmas is gonna be here soon, and the way things are a-looking around here, it ain't gonna be much. Momma told me not to expect a lot, and for her to tell me that when it's right after Thanksgiving means I ain't gonna get nothing. Yeah, I do get a little sad when I think about a Christmas without presents, but you know; I don't care all that much about Christmas presents. Ahaaa, wait a minute, I'm lying like a dog. Yeah, I do want Christmas presents, but since I ain't gonna get none, I just act like everything's okay. But hey, you know what? I've got some good friends, and I like living out here on the farm where I can go in the woods and swamp and roam around. Anyhow, I can't think of a dang thing I really want. Oh, heck, I'm lying again. There's a whole bunch of stuff I want, but I ain't gonna get nothing. So shoot, if I don't get a dang Christmas present it won't matter a whit to me. Liar!

I've tried to save up my paper route money to buy Christmas presents, but Momma made me spend all the money I'd saved up last week for some new school shoes. So today, I've got thirty-five cents to my name. Not much for Momma, Daddy, and John Clayton. Well, there is one more person that I'd like to get a present for, Rosalie. She's without a doubt the prettiest girl in the whole entire school, and I've been real close to being her boyfriend a couple of times, but right now she's just barely speaking to me. If I could get her something she really wants I think she would be my girlfriend. Freckles, Rosalie's best friend, told me a week ago that they'd been in El Dorado shopping, and Rosalie had seen a bright red scarf at Samples Department Store, and she'd just gone on and on about it. Said red was her favorite color, and that she'd give anything to have that scarf. Well, I had decided right then and there, that was gonna be her Christmas present from me. Course that was before I had to spend my paper route money on school shoes. So, here I am about four weeks before Christmas without much hope to come up with the money to buy that red scarf. Heck, the paper route money between now and then won't even be close to enough, course I'll spend about half of it on other stuff.

Oh, I almost forgot about old Uncle Hugh. He lives by hisself in a little one room cabin about a mile off the El Dorado highway. Heck, I might not get much this Christmas, but it'll be a whole lot more than Uncle Hugh gets. He's as poor as Job's turkey. This year, after I stuck the nail in my foot, we started coming by his house a couple of times a week cause Uncle Hugh was having leg problems, and it was hard for him to walk all the way from his house to Norphlet for groceries. We started delivering his groceries the first week in October.

Anyway, I'd sure like to buy some little present for those people, but the way things look right now, if I get them anything it's gonna be real cheap, or I'll end up making some stupid, home-made craft, which is always tacky and everybody will look at it, smile, thank me, and then they'll chunk it way as soon as I'm not around.

3

Bubba and the Roughnecks

Friday, November 24th, 1944

Dang, after fooling around with Sniffer and the big coon fight, I was running late for my paper route. Old Doc, who owns the newsstand, has set fifteen minutes as the late cutoff time, and if I'm one minute later than that, he'll dock my route money fifty cents.

My gosh, and I'm not kidding, if there's anything in the whole blessed entire world I hate, it's that dang paper route during the winter, but shoot, three and a half dollars a week ain't a whole lot of money, but it's a heck of a lot better than nothing, so bad weather or not, I gotta deliver them sorry papers.

I stepped back inside our screened-in back porch, picked up my flashlight, called Sniffer, and started trotting down the road to Norphlet. Well, it didn't take long before I was in downtown Norphlet, my home town. Norphlet is only about 650 people, but it was a whole bunch bigger during the oil boom of the 1920s. It ain't much of a town now. Most of the buildings are vacant, and me and my friends have a lot of fun playing war games in them. Course in a little, dinky town like Norphlet, I know everybody by their first name, and they sure as heck know me, cause I'm their paperboy.

I passed the pool hall, which we call Peg's Place, the Red Star Drug Store, the Post Office, and there, right next to the Post Office, is the City Café. Old Mrs. Martin owns and runs the café, which serves up a great Blue Plate Special usually featuring catfish or buffalo fish caught out of the Ouachita River. Me and Daddy go by there at least once a week to eat catfish. Dang, old Mrs. Martin's fried catfish and hush puppies is so good I can taste them right now. Well, I'll admit the City Café could use a little fixing up cause old Mrs. Martin can't see very good and she lets the café get a little messy, heck, it's more than a little messy, and Momma just shakes her head when Daddy tells her we're going to eat there. Momma ain't about to eat there.

Mrs. Martin is a really old widow woman of about fifty, a kinda large woman, who wears her gray hair in a big bun on the back of her head and never wears no lipstick or nothing. Her old blue checked dress that she wears most every day comes down to her ankles, and she wears rolled-up hose. She has a voice like a foghorn, and when she yells an order from out in the café to Bubba, who is a-cooking back in the kitchen, he can hear her clear as a bell. Momma said Mrs. Martin's Pentecostal, and they don't allow no makeup or nothing like that. However, she does dip snuff and carries a little cup around to spit in, but I guess that's all right with the Pentecostals. Of course the snuff, stale beer, and Bubba frying catfish in the kitchen without no fan, makes the café smell to high heaven, but heck, nobody gives a durn, cause the food's so good.

I smiled and almost laughed out loud, as I looked at the plywood Mrs. Martin had nailed in the windows after the big fight last week. Heck, that brawl, and I'm telling you, it was one of the most exciting things Norphlet has seen in a heck of a long time. Dang, I wish I could've been there instead of just hearing about it. Course the next morning it was all over town—every little detail. My gosh, it must have been really something.

You might know it was some of them sorry oil field roughnecks that started it. Our little town is right in the heart of the south Arkansas oil fields, and although the oil boom has been over for a long time, there's still a bunch of trashy oil field workers around. This past week three of them roughnecks, who work on Mr. Crotty's drilling rig out near Snow Hill, came a-walking into the café right before it closed. Roughnecks is the men that work on the big rigs that drill the oil wells, and they're called roughnecks cause a long time ago they had to carry drill-pipe on their shoulders, and it would scratch up their necks. Daddy said roughnecks are about the meanest and toughest men in the oil fields, and they'll get wound up and start a fight at the drop of a hat. He's durn sure right about that.

The driller, who's the boss of the crew, was a great big man who was way over six feet tall, and I'll bet that guy weighed at least 275 pounds. Everybody around Norphlet knows he's as mean as a snake, and he's always getting into fights. I don't have a clue what his real name is, but everybody calls him Big Six. Course I thought they called him Big Six cause he was big and over six feet tall, but that ain't it. One of the men he works with told Daddy he picked up that nickname when he was a big five-year-old and had two six shooters. How about that?

Well, this sorry bunch had a day off, and they'd been down the street in Peg's Place guzzling beer and raising a ruckus all afternoon. They staggered into the City Café and told Mrs. Martin they wanted a bunch of fried catfish with all the trimming, and for her to hurry up cause they were really hungry. She yelled out to Bubba back in the kitchen.

"Three cats; load 'um up!"

According to some of the other customers the whole bunch was about three sheets to the wind, you know—drunk. Bubba, who had already closed the kitchen, stuck his head out of the kitchen and yelled back at Mrs. Martin.

"Grease is done got cold, and I ain't 'bout to heat it up again!"

Mrs. Martin went back in the kitchen and after a little talk, Bubba stuck his head back out and yelled to the bunch.

"Y'all just hold your horses; it's gonna take a while."

"Better not take long!" yelled Big Six.

Bubba gave them a bad look and then went back in the kitchen. Course since he had to heat the stove and the grease in the deep fat fryer, it took a whole bunch longer and after about ten minutes Big Six started beating his steel hardhat on the table and yelling at Bubba. Pretty soon them other two roughnecks was a-hollering and yelling.

"Hey! You sorry son-of-a-gun! Hurry up! We're hungry! Get your lazy, worthless butt out here with our food!" That's what they was a-saying according to Mrs. Martin, who went over to the table and yelled for them to shut up.

Mrs. Martin was trying to clam them up because she knew Bubba didn't take kindly to nobody yelling at him. You know, I don't know what Bubba's real name is, but everybody in town just calls him Bubba. Heck, Big Six is a big man, but Bubba is something else. He's by far the biggest man in town, and he ain't particularly easy-going, and shoot, you don't dare complain about his cooking. A few years ago Bubba was working as a roughneck on a drilling rig, and when they was a-pulling the drillpipe out of the hole, the pulling chain broke and flew clear across the floor, whacking Bubba longside his head. The story I heard was that Bubba's brains were almost hanging out and everybody was sure he was a goner, but they hauled him off to the hospital and put a steel plate in his head. Bubba's head was so swollen after the operation that people didn't recognize him, but after several weeks the swelling went down and Bubba opened his eyes for the first time since his accident. Well, he talked kinda slurred and later, when he started walking again, he'd throw one foot out to the right and the other to the left. It was a walk like nobody in Norphlet had ever seen, and walking around, talking and swaggering like that, he was plain scary, especially to little kids. Dang, when old Bubba came a-walking down the sidewalk people just scattered. But shoot, Bubba; he ain't mean a-tall. In fact, me and John Clayton are friends of Bubba's, and we come by and talk with him most every day, but lordy mercy; dang, don't make him mad cause oh, my God in heaven above, if he loses his temper, you'd better run like a scalded dog.

Bubba heard them roughnecks a-yelling and barged out the door carrying a big black iron skillet. He was swaying back and forth, walking kinda spraddle-legged, and tobacco juice was dripping out the side of his mouth and you could tell he was getting kinda mad.

"By God!" Bubba yelled. "If I hear one more word from you worthless bunch of trash, I'm gonna clean house with this here skillet!" He waved the skillet over his head and spit tobacco juice in the can he was carrying. Well, them roughnecks was quiet for about ten seconds until Big Six leaned back and started laughing at Bubba.

"Whoooo! Haaaaa! Ha! Ha! You shore a-scarin' me! Now get your dumb butt back in the kitchen and fix us some supper!"

Course that just got them other roughnecks a-going. I guess all that beer they drank down at Peg's Place musta gone to their heads, because all of them started laughing and making fun of Bubba. Then Big Six threw his steel hardhat at him and yelled, "Hit this big fellow! Ha! Ha! Ha! You're all mouth! You mumble-mouth, wobble-legged slob! Now, get your butt back in the kitchen and fix us some supper, or I'm gonna kick it back!" The hardhat sailed across the room and banged against the wall, almost hitting old Bubba.

According to one of the other customers sitting at the bar, when that hardhat hit the wall beside him, Bubba's mouth dropped open, tobacco juice ran out of both sides of his mouth, his eyes crossed, he bared his teeth and let out a roar.

"Ahhhhhhh, you worthless trash! Makin' fun of me! I'll teach you some manners!" Bubba walked over to where Big Six's steel hardhat was lying and swung that skillet at it.

Whap!

Boy, Bubba crushed Big Six's hardhat almost flat and then kicked it like you would a football and it hit Big Six right above the ankle.

Mrs. Martin squealed like a stuck pig cause she durn well knew the place was about to break loose.

"Now, stop it, Bubba! And Big Six, you just calm down!"

Shoot, Mrs. Martin might as well just kept her mouth shut cause there weren't nobody paying no attention to her.

"Ahaaaa! You worthless—" But before Big Six could get up, Bubba kicked the leg of the chair that roughneck was sitting on so hard it broke and sent Big Six sprawling out on the floor. Then Bubba drew back his skillet.

"Ahaaaaaaa! No! Bubba! Don't!" screamed Mrs. Martin.

But Bubba was already drawed back and swinging.

His first swing knocked all three beer bottles off the table. Glass went everywhere, and them other two roughnecks jumped back out of skillet range.

Big Six yelled, "Don't!" just as the second skillet swing whacked him across his shoulder. You could hear the thud of the skillet when it hit Big Six's shoulder all the way across the café. My Lord, people started a-yelling and a-hollering and everybody but them roughnecks started running for the door, as Bubba tossed his coffee can full of tobacco juice across the room and drew back to whop Big Six again.

Mrs. Martin let out a high-pitched scream that you could've heard a mile away and slapped old Bubba across the back to try and get him to stop. Heck, Bubba paid about as much attention to Mrs. Martin as he would a mosquito.

"Now, I'm gonna teach you a thing or two!" Bubba stood over Big Six, who was really hurting from the skillet swat on the shoulder, and drawed back the skillet. Mrs. Martin was trying to hold on to Bubba, but she weren't doing no good, and Big Six, he was a-trying to crawl away as Bubba started to whap him again. Bubba was gonna whap Big Six right on the top of his head. Course if he had, old Big Six would be dead as a doorknob right now.

"Help! Help! Don't hit me again!" Big Six was a-hollering as he tried to crawl away. About that time them other two rough-necks decided to get into the fight.

"Git 'em!" yelled one of the other roughnecks as they rushed Bubba, and before Bubba could swing, they tackled him.

"Ahhhhhhhhh!" Bubba screamed and slapped one of the men halfway across the room with his free hand and started after the other with the skillet. Big Six finally got up off the floor, jumped on Bubba's back, and tried to choke him, but he didn't even slow Bubba down. It was one of the dangdest fights you ever did see. Bubba trying to corner one of the other roughnecks while Big Six was riding his back, and the other roughneck, the one Bubba had knocked across the room, was trying to hit Bubba with a beer bottle, while old Mrs. Martin ran round the café waving her hands over her head and screaming like nothing you've ever heard.

Bubba trapped the roughneck he was chasing in a corner, and in spite of Big Six choking him and the other roughneck hitting him with a beer bottle, scored another hit, this time right in the middle of the roughneck's back, as he tried to keep from being trapped in a corner.

Well, by now the café was just going crazy with screaming customers, yelling roughnecks, and Bubba, who figured his skillet was gonna clean house. Bubba still had Big Six on his back, trying to choke him, and was chasing the other two around the café, knocking over chairs and scaring customers when he and Big Six fell right in the middle of a table. Dang, when about seven hundred pounds hit that table, glasses, plates, and wood splinters went a-flying.

About that time Mrs. Martin, who had been running around screaming, trying to stop the fight, ran outside yelling at the top of her lungs, "Call the law! Call the law!" She looked around and spotted City Constable Curly Sawyer, who was coming out of Peg's Place about half drunk. Curly, who pretty much stays a little drunk, when he's not sleeping in the chair down at his office, wobbled down the street toward a screaming Mrs. Martin.

"Curly! Hurry up and get in there and stop that fight! They're a-tearing up my café!" she yelled.

"What? What?" said Curly, who looked a little confused and staggered across the street the opposite way from the café with Mrs. Martin right behind him, yelling her head off.

You know, Curly's not much of a constable. Daddy told me he's the laziest man he's ever known, and I guess Daddy's right, cause I've never seen old Curly do nothing but drink beer in Peg's Place. Course all that drinking keeps his face as red as Santa Claus, and his big nose almost glows. Curly's not very tall, but he has one of the biggest bellies in town, and it hangs over his belt like a big oversize tire. He lives in a little three-room shotgun shack out on the edge of town with a woman who everybody says is not his wife.

Wife or not, they've got thirteen kids, and if it wasn't for the church folks, they'd starve to death.

Mrs. Martin, who was still screaming that the fight was a-tearing up her café, grabbed Curly, who was a little groggy and moving in the wrong direction, and slapped him across the shoulder to get his attention.

"Dang it, Curly! Do something!" she yelled right in his face. "They're in the café! The café!" she screamed and pointed across the street.

"Oh, yeah; the café, yeah." Curly nodded as he stumbled toward the café from across the street.

"I'm gettin' right on it, Mrs. Martin. I'll take care of this bunch of sorry trash!" He drew his pistol and stumbled through the door waving his big .45, yelling at the top of his lungs, "You in there! Stop that fightin'! Stop! Y'all's under arrest!"

According to Mrs. Martin, Bubba still had the skillet in his hand and was swinging at anybody in range. One of the roughnecks had picked up a chair leg and was trying to fend off Bubba while Big Six, who was dodging the skillet, tried to hit Bubba. Curly had no more gotten the "*Stop the fightin'!*" words out of his mouth, when Big Six snatched up a beer bottle and chunked it at him. That beer bottle caught old Curly longside his head and broke into a million pieces.

"Ahaaaa! Oh! Oh! By God, you're gonna regret that!" Curly screamed as he staggered back out the door into the street, cursing at the top of his lungs as blood trickled down the side of his head. "I'll teach you worthless bunch of trash a thing or two!" he screamed, wiping the blood off his face. With that, he turned around, cocked his gun and started firing. Heck, Mrs. Martin said Curly weren't shooting at nothing in particular, he was just aiming at the café and by gollee, Mrs. Martin, she went plum crazy as glass started shattering.

"My café! My café!" She was yelling as she hopped around, waving her hands.

Curly shot out both front plate glass windows, the door

window, and most of the glasses sitting on the bar before he ran out of shells. When the shooting started, everyone in the café hit the floor, and when the smoke cleared they couldn't believe that not one person had been hit. Curly staggered in and arrested the whole bunch, but since Norphlet ain't got no jail, he let them go with only a warning and made them pay Mrs. Martin for the broken windows and table.

As they were leaving, Big Six shook his fist at Bubba and yelled at him, "Hey, you big wobble-legged slob! We're gonna get your behind! Next time we'll see how tough you are! I'm gonna beat you to a pulp!"

"Come on back any time, and I'll beat the fool outta you with this skillet!" yelled Bubba as he shook his skillet at him.

"That's enough!" yelled Curly, who had now reloaded He fired his gun in the air, and everybody scattered.

"Dang you, Curly, you worthless so-in-so; now I've got a hole in my ceilin'!" yelled Mrs. Martin. She shooed Curly out the door before he could fire another round.

The next morning after the big shootout, me and John Clayton stopped by the café to check out the damage, and there was Bubba a-cleaning up the mess. Shoot, the story about the fight and Curly's shooting had gotten all over town. John Clayton stuck his head in the door of the café.

"Bubba."

"What you want?"

"Well, Bubba, we heard you really cleaned house with that skillet."

Bubba, who was wearing a Red Man baseball cap, chewing on a toothpick on one side of his mouth, and had a plug of tobacco in the other side of his mouth, smiled and walked over to the door where we were standing.

"Dang right, I done cleaned house, and if old drunk Curly Sawyer hadn't shot things up, I'd have finished the job." He leaned back against the door and spit in the coffee can he was carrying.

"Heck, Bubba, I heard Big Six yelled at you after the fight was over that he was gonna get you," I said. "He's really tough. Ain't you 'fraid of 'em?"

"Huh, let him come back. I'll use that skillet on 'em again."

"Bubba, what kinda skillet did you use?"

"I used that old, black skillet that I fry bacon in. Y'all come on in, and I'll show you." We walked in the café with Bubba, stepping over broken bottles, chair legs, and trash.

"This is it!" He waved a big black skillet over his head. "I done drawed back like this—and whap! And then—"

Me and John Clayton started backing out the door cause Mrs. Martin was walking in from the kitchen.

"Bubba, if I ever see you swing that skillet again, I'm gonna bend it over your stupid head!" She screamed in her loudest foghorn voice as she spit snuff in her little cup and shook her fist at Bubba.

Bubba looked like he'd been shot.

4

Doc, the Newsstand, and My Paper Route

Friday, November 24th, 1944

Doc Rollinson's newsstand is right beside the City Café, and when I got to the door I could see old Doc a-sitting in his wheelchair reading the paper. Dang, I could see Doc frowning from plum out on the sidewalk. Shoot, that frown never leaves his face, but heck, if I was stuck in a wheelchair all day long, I'd be grumpy as an old wet hen too.

That north wind had dropped the temperature to almost freezing, and I was shaking by the time I got into the newsstand. Sniffer plopped down beside the door, and I walked in trying to come up with an excuse for being over fifteen minutes late. I stepped through the door into a fog of cigarette smoke and brushed off a place on the old crosscut pine floor where I could sit down and roll my papers.

"Hi, Doc, sorry I'm late." I looked up at Doc from the floor where I was sitting, and then I thought about Sniffer and the fight with the big coon, and I decided that'd be a good excuse. "But me and Sniffer had to chase a big old coon outta the chicken house, and it took a bunch longer cause of the big fight."

Doc looked up from reading the paper; scowling. "Bull!" He put the paper down and looked at the big clock over his desk.

"Hmmm; twenty minutes late. That's gonna cost ya a fiftycent deduction from this week's route money. Richard, that's a sorry excuse. Can't you do bettern that? Dumb lazy kids; never wanta work," he mumbled.

Well, that's Doc Rollinson, the newsstand owner, who was in an oil-field accident a long time ago and got his legs crushed. Last month Doc started using a cigarette holder when he smokes, cause he thinks when he rolls around in that old wheelchair with his teeth clamped down on that cigarette holder he looks kinda like President Roosevelt. Only Doc thinks that. He's seventy, cranky, and always believing I'm making up excuses for being late. I'll hafta admit; most of the time he's right, but heck, Doc's not a bad person a-tall, just grumpy.

"Doc, it's the God's truth if I've ever told it; I promise, cross my heart, and hope to die."

"Oh, come on, Richard; you made up that stuff 'bout Sniffer. Gimme one good reason why I should believe you, and not dock you fifty cents for being late!"

Shoot, I thought old Doc had me, but then I thought about Sniffer rubbing his chewed-up ear against the steps.

"Well, Doc, Sniffer and the coon really did get into one heck of a fight, and I'll bet Sniffer has some coon bites on his head or ears."

"Ha! Baloney!" Doc made a little mark on my time card and picked his paper back up.

"Okay, Doc, we'll see." I opened the door and called Sniffer. "Here, Sniffer, here, come here."

Sniffer stuck his head in the door of the newsstand, wondering why I was calling him to come in a place he'd been run out of so many times.

"Come on, Sniffer," I said as I clapped my hands.

Sniffer trotted in, and I held his head up for Doc.

Doc glanced over the top of his paper at Sniffer and nodded his head.

"My gosh, Richard, you're right. Sniffer's ear is all chewed up."

"Yeah, Doc, it was so dark I couldn't see how bad that coon bit Sniffer when it happened. I'll put some medicine on it when I get home."

"Well, maybe you and Sniffer did run some old coon out of

your chicken house before you came downtown. I won't deduct anything this time. It musta been one big coon to whip Sniffer."

"Yeah, Doc, and you ain't never heard so much squallin' and howlin' as they were makin'."

"Okay, Richard; I believe you; now get those dang papers rolled and in your bag. Oh, yeah, Mr. Cheers said it was ten after six yesterday before he got his paper. You'd better have a paper on everybody's porch by six o'clock, or you're gonna get that deduct. Now get that smelly dog outta this newsstand. He's stinkin' up the place."

"Yes, sir."

Well, the dang paper route was terrible. Walking along with my flashlight at five-thirty in the morning into a strong north wind with it misting rain is about as bad as it gets. I talked to Sniffer almost the whole way, and he'd shake his head and howl as I complained. It was weather not fit for boy or dog. I made it back home a little after six o'clock, fed the chickens and mules, and walked in the kitchen to have breakfast. I was so cold my fingers were numb and my legs were shaking.

When I walked in the kitchen from the barn, Daddy was sitting at the kitchen table, drinking a cup of coffee, listening to Walter Winchell, the famous newscaster, give the news about the war. Heck, ever since them danged Japs bombed us, Daddy just stays glued to the radio.

"Richard, what was the racket out in the chicken house before you left for your paper route?"

I backed up to the stove to warm up and said, "Sniffer and a big old coon were goin' after it. There was the biggest dang coon you can ever imagine in the chicken house, and I let Sniffer in to get 'em. But guess what?"

"What?"

"The coon done whipped old Sniffer, and ran him outta the chicken house."

"Whipped Sniffer? That's hard to believe. Last year when he caught one in the garden, he finished it off in no time a-tall."

"Yeah, Daddy; this coon had to be one big rascal." I sat down at the breakfast table and started buttering a couple of biscuits.

Daddy poured himself another cup of coffee and passed me the bacon. I looked at Daddy, who was leaning back in his chair, kidding with Momma, and enjoying his second cup off coffee. It sure didn't look like the same person who was in the living room screaming and yelling at Momma Friday night.

Daddy's hard to figure out. During the week he's great around the house, and even helps me do my chores. However, he is just the opposite on weekends. Friday afternoon's payday, and Daddy heads for Peg's pool hall or Shug's Place out on the El Dorado highway. I don't understand what happens at all. Daddy'll go in, sit down, and order a beer. In twenty minutes he'll order another one, and then another, and soon he'll start buying beer for everyone in the pool hall, and before long he's loaning them money. Heck, I'm only eleven years old, but I can dang sure see where all of Daddy's money goes. Daddy's the big problem with Christmas money. Payday—Peg's pool hall and Daddy's sorry friends send Daddy home broke. Dang, if we didn't raise most of our stuff to eat out here on the farm, we'd starve.

Course I think Daddy's good looking, but I'm his son. However, Mrs. Echols, down at the grocery store, told me last year that all the war widows who work at the refinery think he's the best looking man in town. He has sandy red hair, deep blue eyes, and a great smile. He weighs 190 pounds and is six feet tall. Maybe there's some hope for skinny me.

5

School, Friends, and Enemies

Monday, November 27th, 1944

Wow, that cold north wind kept blowing all weekend, and on Monday morning, after I finished breakfast, I put my winter jacket on and walked to school, bending my head into that freezing wind. By the time I got to school I was more than ready to sit in a warm room. I sit right beside John Clayton. John Clayton is a little shorter than I am, and he weighs about fifteen pounds more than I do. He's got curly black hair which he keeps cut short so people won't think he's a girl. We do everything together.

Rosalie sits right in front of me, and her light blue eyes just melt me when she looks at me. Last fall we were almost boy- and girlfriend, but after getting mad and calling me and John Clayton white trash cause we got sick riding a carnival ride and threw up all over her, she'll barely speak to me. Gosh, I still can't keep my eyes off Rosalie, cause she's so pretty. But I remember sitting there looking at Rosalie that morning just thinking about what I could do to get her to like me again. Then it hit me; *Yeah,* I thought, *Christmas is comin' up, and I'll buy her somethin' special.* Then I frowned as I thought about not having any money. But shoot, it was still a whole month 'til Christmas, so I thought I was bound to come up with some money by then. But, you know, as I think back on it, I really didn't believe that.

John Clayton was still outside when Rosalie turned around, holding her math homework.

"Richard, what did you get on problem seven?"

I was surprised when she spoke and I mumbled, "Uh, well, I'm gonna do the math homework right after the spellin' test."

She gave me one of those looks; you know; like, *There ain't no way.* "You can't finish all the math homework after the spelling test. You'll only have five minutes."

"Well, maybe you could help me a little bit." I wanted to take those words back as soon as they came out of my mouth. Rosalie cheating? She wouldn't have cheated if God in heaven had told her to.

"Help you?" She pulled her head back and glared.

"Yeah, give me an answer or two." I figured I was in deep trouble anyway so why not ask, now that I'd opened my big mouth. Boy, was that another stupid mistake.

Rosalie gave me one of those *get lost* stares, turned up her nose, and whirled back around.

Well, Richard, that was one of the stupidest dang things you could've said, I thought. Heck, I knew Rosalie wouldn't cheat if it meant her life. *Now, I've made her mad again. Well, let's see how much math homework I was supposed to do. Dang it! Get busy.* I pulled my math book out and opened it to the homework page. "Dang, oh, for cryin' out loud," I muttered as I scanned the twenty or so problems.

I'd finished two of them when Mrs. Smith walked into class as the bell sounded. The rest of the class filed in and by the time everybody settled down, I'd completed three more.

The spelling test came next and I whizzed through it, putting down the first thing that came to mind. I grabbed the math book again, and by the time Mrs. Smith took up the spelling test, I'd knocked out three more. I kicked John Clayton, who always had his homework, and motioned for him to pass me some answers. I pointed to number eight. John Clayton looked over at me, nodded, and scribbled something down. His hand slipped out, and I took a note from him. Starting at problem eight, he'd put down the last twelve answers, which I copied as Mrs. Smith called for the math problems to be turned in.

Rosalie looked back, sure I wasn't even going to turn in any homework. When I started to hand it in, I opened it, showing her it was complete. John Clayton snickered, and she glanced at him, figuring out the little scheme. She could've bitten nails she was so mad. *Well, you idiot; you've made her even madder,* I thought. *What's the matter with you?*

I looked back to see if my other good friends, Ears and Tiny, had turned in any homework. Ears, who is tall and skinny with two ears the size of saucers, gave me a choking sign like he was dying, and I knew he didn't turn anything in. Tiny was all smiles so I figured he'd turned something in, and God, yuck; sitting right behind Tiny on the back row, was that sorry, worthless Homer Ray Parks, who sneered and shook his fist at me. Homer Ray, the class bully, is one sorry kid, and I hate his guts. After I got even with him a couple of months ago by pelting him with my slingshot, my daddy warned his daddy that if Homer Ray ever touched me again he'd whip up on him. Course since Daddy weighs 190 pounds to Homer Ray's daddy's 140 pounds, it wouldn't be much of a fight. Homer Ray is as mean as a slimy snake, and he's always torment-ing some of my friends, since he can't pick on me. I knew right then and there that I'd hafta deal with that sorry rascal again.

The rest of the day went about as usual with Mrs. Smith call-ing me down a couple of times for daydreaming. Dang, I don't mind the calling down, but when she cracks me on the head with her ruler, it hurts like heck.

Course the weather man had gotten our hopes up this morn-ing when he said there was a chance of snow late today, but our class of sixth graders all knew any decent snow wasn't gonna hap-pen in November. Heck, it almost never snows here in south Arkansas, even in January or February.

Class was almost over when I glanced out the window for the fortieth time, and for a minute I thought I saw a snowflake, and then, *Yes!* It was snowing; big, fluffy flakes. I poked John Clayton and pointed to the window. Then a murmur swept across the class as everybody spotted the snow. Mrs. Smith rapped her ruler to get everybody's attention, but with it snowing outside, she didn't have a prayer of a chance. I thought we'd have a big snow, and it would cover south Arkansas like a big, white blanket; would last for days and days, and we'd get out of school for a week. In a few minutes the dismissal bell rang, we stood up, and marched out of class down the long hall and through the big double doors running out in the snowstorm shouting.

"Boy, Richard, it's comin' down, and look; it's stickin'! We ain't gonna have no school for a week!" hollered John Clayton.

"Yeah, if it keeps this up we're gonna have snow up to our knees."

"Hey, Richard, it's Monday. Remember, we gotta go to the grocery store for Uncle Hugh."

"Uh, huh, I almost forgot. Well, let's get goin'. It'll be fun walkin' over to Uncle Hugh's house in the snow."

We were still talking about Uncle Hugh as we headed for the grocery store.

"Richard, how old is Uncle Hugh?"

"Heck, he's the oldest colored man I know. In fact, he's the oldest man colored or white I know. I bet he's at least eighty-five."

"Shoot, I think he's almost a hunnerd."

"A hundred? You're crazy, John Clayton. He may be eighty-five or ninety, but he ain't a hundred."

"How do you know? Uncle Hugh told us a few weeks ago he wasn't sure when he was born."

"Well, it doesn't make a whit of difference, does it? He's old as Methuselah, and he needs someone to help him get groceries."

"Yeah, and you know something, Richard? Uncle Hugh's havin' some other problems."

"Maybe it's old age. Daddy said when people gets old, stuff quits workin', and when enough stuff quits workin', you die."

"I don't know, Richard. That may be part of Uncle Hugh's problems, but there's somethin' else. Watch him real close when we get there."

"Oh, dang it! It's stopped snowin'," I said.

"Yeah, I guess we ain't gonna be snowed in this week. At least we can go in to the picture show at the Ritz Saturday," said John Clayton.

We walked up Main Street passing the Red Star Drug Store and Doc's Newsstand, and turned the corner as we passed Camel's Dry Goods. In the next block was Echols Grocery.

We walked in and went to the counter where Mrs. Echols was sitting on a stool writing up charge tickets. She looked up and smiled.

"Boys, what can I do for y'all today?"

"We're shoppin' for Hugh Burns, Mrs. Echols. He wants a tin of shortnin', a loaf of bread, and two pounds of bacon," I said.

"Boys, y'all are sweet to help old Hugh out. Tell him there's a little piece of candy in his sack from me."

"Yes ma'am, but Mrs. Echols, we're a-helpin' Hugh 'cause he's our good friend. Gosh, he's told us a million stories over the last few years. Gettin' these groceries for him ain't much trouble," said John Clayton.

"Well, it's still a sweet thing to do."

Mrs. Echols walked to the back of the store and in a few minutes she was back with a small sack of groceries.

"Here's your sack, and tell Hugh I said hi."

"Yes ma'am," we both said.

6

Our Friend, Uncle Hugh

Monday, November 27th, 1944

We hightailed it out of town and soon we were crossing an old field that had several chinkapin trees scattered around the edge of the field.

"Hey, John Clayton, let's go pick some chinkapins before we go to Uncle Hugh's."

"Okay, let's climb that big tree over in the far corner. We were by there last week, and there was still some up toward the top."

Shoot, by the time we got to the tree both of us were freezing cold, and after we climbed up close to the top, where a few chinkapins were left, we took a good look at each other. We were standing there hanging on a cold limb with a north wind whipping through our hair, hoping we wouldn't fall out before we froze to death.

"Dang! Forget about chinkapins!" I yelled.

"Yeah, let's get down. My fingers are numb," said John Clayton. "I can't believe you wanted to do somethin' this stupid."

"Bull corn! You wanted to do it as much as I did."

"Shoot, who cares? Come on; I'll race you to Uncle Hugh's."

We hit the ground running, heading for Uncle Hugh's and his warm fireplace, but before we got there we got tired of running and we slowed down and trudged up the little dirt lane past the spring where Uncle Hugh gets his water. We could smell the smoke from his fireplace before we could see his cabin.

Uncle Hugh lives a mile from town, and with the detour to get chinkapins and walking with the cold north wind blowing in our faces, we were more than ready to warm up in front of a roaring fire.

He was standing on his front porch waving to us when we walked up.

"Uncle Hugh, how you doin'?" I hollered.

"Jus' fine boys, but this here north wind is gettin' a little cold. I think we needs to go in by the fireplace, if we's gonna talk very long."

Uncle Hugh had on his old brown coat that one of the ladies at the church gave him, and his tattered railroad cap was pulled down over his ears. Course he was smiling just as he was every time we visited. Gosh, for somebody just barely getting by, Uncle Hugh is sure a surprise cause he's always happy. I ain't never heard him complain about nothing.

"Yeah, Uncle Hugh, we were gonna go pick chinkapins, but we chickened out cause it was so cold," I said. "We're freezin'."

"Let me get to that fireplace!" yelled John Clayton. He bolted though the door and was backed up to the fireplace when me and Uncle Hugh walked in.

Uncle Hugh had put extra wood on the fire right before we arrived, and them crackling oak limbs were giving off a bunch of heat. Gosh, it felt so good to stand there and warm up in front of his big fireplace.

Uncle Hugh followed us in and sat down in his rocking chair, and we plopped down on the floor beside the fireplace. The fireplace had the cabin good and warm, and the coal oil lantern gave off a soft glow. It felt so cozy to be there in front of the fireplace with that north wind blowing and rattling the tin roof on Uncle Hugh's little cabin.

We've known Uncle Hugh for about three years, and we've stopped by his little cabin a bunch of times, but after I got the nail in my foot, we've gotten to be real good friends.

I took a good look at Uncle Hugh when he followed us in and started for the rocking chair. Uncle Hugh's a good sized man, and although he's not as tall as Daddy, he probably weighs a little more. His skin is a dark, dusty black, he has only has a few gray hairs left on his head, but he's still got the biggest mouthful of the whitest teeth I've ever seen. Uncle Hugh had his nose broken when he was working for the railroad, when a boxcar door banged him across the face. It left his nose slightly bent. He has two big creases on either side of his nose, but other than that, his face is smooth as a baby's.

Uncle Hugh worked for the railroad until he retired over twenty years ago. He's always talking about his railroad job, which he said was the best job he ever had. The railroad folks gave him a gold watch when he retired, and of course it's Uncle Hugh's prize possession. Every time we come over, he makes a big show of pulling the gold chain up from his pocket, holding the watch out in front of him, opening the little gold face, and pronouncing the time.

His railroad retirement check is fifty-five dollars a month, which ain't enough for him to get by on. Toward the end of the month his grocery list is down to just a few little things, and me and John Clayton add to his sack, telling him we got the stuff on sale. Last week adding to Uncle Hugh's grocery list took half of my paper route money, and all of John Clayton's fifty-cent-a-week allowance.

Uncle Hugh's a good friend, but the reason we visit with him and sometime sit around for hours, is to hear stories about the olden days when Uncle Hugh was a little boy, or stories his mother told him about slave times, and how after being freed, she walked all the way from the Delta to El Dorado.

His cabin's great. The tin-covered plank porch goes across the front of the cabin, and sitting back against the wall is a big rocking chair. When we visit during the summer, Uncle Hugh sits in the rocking chair, and me and John Clayton will plop down anywhere. In the summer the wood porch floor feels cool on our bare backs, and Sniffer will lie in front of Uncle Hugh to get his back rubbed with Uncle Hugh's bare feet. When the weather gets cold, he drags the rocking chair in from the porch and everybody sits around the big fireplace. The fireplace is all the heat Uncle Hugh has except for the cast iron cookstove. He has a little dining table over on one side of the room, and his bed is on the other side.

Uncle Hugh's proud he can read and write. Before he worked for the railroad, he worked at a sawmill, and the man that owned the mill taught Uncle Hugh how to read and write during the winter, when the mill was shut down. When we're inside and sitting around the fire, he'll light the coal oil lantern, take the Bible, and read to us. Usually, it's out of Proverbs and has something to do with young boys growing up.

Uncle Hugh never gets nothing for Christmas, except for a little food basket from the A.M.E. church. Last year I asked him what A.M.E. stood for, and he said it was for African Methodist Episcopalian Church.

"Boys, y'all's mighty good to bring me these here groceries, 'specially in this bad weather."

"Oh, it ain't much trouble. If we went straight home from school, our daddies would put us to work. I'd dang sure rather sit here by the fire and talk to you," I said.

"Here's your change, and Mrs. Echols said to tell you hi. She put a little piece of candy in the sack."

"Well, thank y'all again, boys, and tell Mrs. Echols hello, and that I really appreciates the candy." He reached out for his change, which I was trying to hand to him, but he was missing my hand. I looked at John Clayton and nodded. Uncle Hugh couldn't see worth a darn. After we were with him a while longer, and as we watched him try to put up his groceries and get around the cabin, I could tell he was almost blind.

Finally, I looked at him and said, "Uncle Hugh, I ain't seen you readin' the Bible lately."

He mumbled something, and I asked. "Are you havin' problems seein'?"

He hesitated for a couple of minutes, and then he said; "Boys, I shore is. 'Bout a year ago my eyes started gettin' worse and worse, and I ain't been able to read the Bible for a long time, and it's even gettin' hard to cook and do stuff 'round this cabin."

"Heck, Uncle Hugh, you need to go see an eye doctor. I bet you need glasses," said John Clayton.

"Boys, y'all knows I can't go to El Dorado. I can barely get to Norphlet, and the thought of ridin' a train over and havin' to stay all day wears me out. Anyway, I ain't got no money for glasses. My railroad pension is barely 'nough to buy groceries."

"Heck, Uncle Hugh, we're goin' to El Dorado on Saturday to see a picture show. We'll go by the eye doctor's office, and see about gettin' you some glasses," I said.

"Yeah," said John Clayton. "Shoot, we'll have you some glasses by this time next week."

"Now, boys, y'all don't worry none 'bout me, I's makin' it jus' fine."

"Okay, Uncle Hugh, but we'll check it out anyway. Heck, it probably ain't hard to get glasses," said John Clayton.

"Say, boys, y'all said you was gonna get chinkapins when you stopped by here. Is you gettin' many chinkapins this year?"

"Shoot, yes, the trees were loaded down. I've never seen so many," said John Clayton.

Uncle Hugh nodded his head and said, "I thought so. I's noticed all them acorns on that pin oak in the back yard, and that old hickory tree out front is jus' full of hicker' nuts. Y'all know what that means?"

"No, what?" We both said.

"Boys, it means we's gonna have a hard winter, and to be sure, I cut open a persimmon seed, and sure 'nough the sprout inside looked like a knife."

"Huh?" I said.

"That's right, a knife; means a cuttin' winter. Wind that'll cut you down, blowin' right outta the north all winter long. Y'all knows we don't usually have this kinda wind this early in the winter. It's gonna be the coldest winter in a long time, and y'all can count on it."

"Really?"

"Boys, even the almanac says it."

We sat there talking about a cold winter and Uncle Hugh told us about the winter of 1878, when the snow was two feet deep right here in south Arkansas, and a big red wolf got in his chicken yard. Uncle Hugh was just about our age and that dang wolf almost got him.

"Is it gonna snow this year, Uncle Hugh?"

"Richard, it shore is, and not just a little dustin'. We's gonna see a real snow, and maybe more'n one."

"Oh boy!" It was the best news we'd had in a long time, and heck, coming from Uncle Hugh, we knew it was true. We were enjoying our visit and had lost track of time when I turned and looked out the window.

"Dang, John Clayton, it's gettin' late. I told Ears and Tiny we'd meet 'um at the breadbox; let's go. Sniffer! Here, Sniffer."

"Yeah, see you, Uncle Hugh," said John Clayton as we darted out the door.

"We'll see you next Sunday to pick up your grocery list," I yelled as I jumped from the top step of the porch and headed out the gate.

7

A Great Plan to
Make Christmas Money

Monday, November 27th, 1944

We made it to Echols Grocery in a few minutes, hopped up on top of the breadbox, and leaned back against the store to get out of the wind. It wasn't long before Tiny and Ears walked up. Ears started just going on and on about his uncle from Hibank, a little town over in eastern Union County, who's fighting the Germans. Course Ears's uncle ain't no big deal; he just drives a truck in the army, and I have two uncles that's actually shooting Germans. One of 'em has been shot in the knee, so I can top anything Ears has to say about the war. So there we sit, talking about mostly nothing, and trying to come up with something to do.

We were still talking about the war and how soon the sorry Germans would be surrendering when Rosalie walked up. Everybody said hi, and Rosalie spoke, but she made a point of speaking to everyone but me. She was still all hacked off about this morning math homework.

After Rosalie walked into the store, John Clayton looked at me and said, "Oh, hi, Richard, the invisible boy."

Everybody had a good laugh since it was obvious Rosalie was acting like I weren't even there.

"Richard, the invisible boy; ha, ha," hooted John Clayton.

"Ah, who cares 'bout Rosalie? She's stuck up anyway," I said as I tried to make excuses, but I was thinking how pretty she looked, and was really kinda bothered that she didn't speak to me.

I've gotta do something special for her, I thought. *Christmas; yeah, Christmas. Somethin' really special for Christmas—the red scarf...*

We laughed and talked for a little while longer, and then we made plans to meet Saturday at the Ritz Theater in El Dorado to see a picture show.

Saturday, December 2nd, 1944

The next Saturday morning, before we went to the picture show in El Dorado, I met John Clayton down at the Red Star Drug Store. It had rained most of the night, and there was a cold mist in the air as the wind changed from the southeast to northwest. We rushed in the drug store to get warm and have a Coca-Cola just as Mr. Tommy Benton, a friend that works with Daddy at the refinery, walked in carrying his mail.

"Hey, boys; cold 'nough for ya?"

"Yes, sir. I dang near froze to death deliverin' papers this mornin'."

"Well, this cold weather is shore good for my business; makes them coons and minks put on a good heavy fur," he said and started opening his mail.

Mr. Benton buys and sells fur to make a little extra money, and since we spend so much time in Flat Creek Swamp, he's always after us to bring him coon skins and other fur. However, we ain't very good at catching nothing but possums. Sometimes, someone will run over a big old coon on the highway and we'll take it over to Mr. Benton, but other than that we don't sell him very much.

Daddy told me that until a few years ago, Mr. Benton stayed down on the river and made a living by trotlining for catfish and making moonshine. When the sheriff found his moonshine still and busted it up, he came into town and managed to get a job at the refinery.

Well, Mr. Benton is quite a character around town cause he's one of the few men we know with a full beard, and he braids the back of his hair like an Indian. He tells everybody he's half

Cherokee, but a few years ago when he was about half drunk he told Daddy that he didn't have an ounce of Indian blood in him; he just liked to be different. He's just an old river rat that was forced into town; at least that's what I think. Well, he sure looks the part with his weather-worn, dark brown, wrinkled face, and I've never seen Mr. Benton when he didn't have his pipe in his mouth. Most of the time it's not even lit, but it's part of the way Mr. Benton talks, as he takes his pipe in one hand and waves it around, punching out each point that he's trying to make. I'm not sure he could say anything if you took away his pipe. Anyway, Mr. Benton's friendly to us, and he's always giving us advice about the swamps and woods.

We sat down and searched through our pocket, looking for enough money to buy a Coca-Cola. John Clayton loaned me two cents to make a nickel, and we bought our drinks. As we sat there sipping our drinks, we started going over every possible way to make extra money for Christmas presents. I would have a few weeks of paper route money, but I knew something would come up to cut into that, or more likely, I'd spend about half on stuff for school or picture shows and candy, so at best, I'd have about four dollars when Christmas rolled around. The idea of getting Rosalie the red scarf as a Christmas present crossed my mind about that time, and I shook my head. Heck, I needed some serious Christmas money, if I was gonna buy that red scarf. It didn't look very promising and John Clayton, who didn't have a job, but got a fifty-cent-a-week allowance, was about in the same shape. We were moaning about not having any money when Mr. Benton, who had overheard us talking, waved a sheet of paper at us.

"Boys, if y'all want to make some money, take a look at this." He handed a paper over to me. "It's the latest fur prices, and they're up a bunch," he said, tapping his pipe stem on the paper.

I took the paper, and me and John Clayton started reading it.

"Dang, Richard, they're paying up to twenty dollars for a female mink skin."

"Yeah, and seven-fifty for a big coon."

"Boys, y'all are always roamin' 'round in Flat Creek Swamp. Shoot, that place is full of coons and maybe a few mink. Richard, didn't old man Davis give you his huntin' dog?"

"Yes, sir."

"Y'all autta take that dog down to the swamp and catch you a sack full of those big old coons. You'd have plenty of Christmas money then." He pointed to the line on the paper that said, RACCOONS—$7.50.

"Yeah, Richard, let's take old Sniffer and do some coon huntin'," said John Clayton, who was starting to see dollar signs.

"Uh, well, uh, Sniffer hunts okay, but all he ever trees are possums. How much do possum skins bring?"

John Clayton ran his finger down the page 'til he came to OPOSSUMS.

"Here—twenty-five."

"Wow, twenty-five dollars for a possum skin?"

"Naw, boys, that's twenty-five cents. Not much demand for possums. But if you can't catch coons or mink, you can at least catch rabbits. For some reason rabbit fur is in demand this year, and I can pay three-fifty apiece for a good hide."

"Really? Gosh, there are a lot of rabbits around our farm, but Daddy won't let me have a gun 'til I'm fourteen. It's hard to get rabbits without a gun."

"Oh, I won't buy rabbit skins with no gunshot holes in 'um. Y'all need to trap 'um."

"I guess rabbits are out, cause we can't afford steel traps."

"Boys, y'all don't need no steel trap to catch rabbits. You need a box rabbit trap."

"What's a box rabbit trap?"

"Come here, and I'll show you." Mr. Benton clamped down on the stem of his pipe, took out a pencil from his pocket, and started to draw on a napkin.

"It's real simple. You build a long box big 'nough for a rabbit to crawl in, and make a slidin' door on one end and close up the other. Next, you cut a hole about three-fourths of the way down on top of the box; big enough to stick a one-inch stick with a notch cut four inches from the bottom of the stick into the box. Then build a little bridge in the middle of the box about eight inches high; take another stick as long as the box, tie the notched stick to one end and the sliding door to the other. Make the string long enough to where when the notched stick is in the end of the box the other end pulls up the sliding door. Put a trail of corn up to the box and a bunch of corn back in the end, and when the rabbit follows the corn into the box, he'll have to push the stick outta the way to get to the corn in the back of the box. When the rabbit does that the stick will slip out of the notch, fly straight up, and the sliding door will drop down, and you've got a four-dollar rabbit."

"Four dollars?" I questioned.

"Yeah, three-fifty for the rabbit skin, and don't forget, you can sell the rabbit's meat for at least fifty cents, but remember, always leave the left hind foot on the skinned rabbit, so folks'll know it's a rabbit, not a little dog."

"Little dog?"

"Yeah, boys; times is shore hard and some trash will do anything to make a little money."

"You mean kill, skin, and sell a little dog and call it a rabbit?" I said.

"Yep."

I looked at John Clayton and he looked at me as we thought the same thing. Last fall a boy just a little older than us stopped by our house selling skinned rabbits and Momma bought one. John Clayton had supper with us that night and we both said how funny that rabbit tasted.

"Richard, that wasn't a little dog; was it?"

"*Roooff*," I said, and we both cracked up.

Mr. Benton turned back to his paper, and me and John Clayton started going back over the plan to make a rabbit trap. It seemed too easy.

I'm not kidding you; in my mind I could see dollar bills just hopping around our farm.

"Wow, that's sounds great. Come on, John Clayton, we can get some boards and work on the rabbit trap in our barn. We can catch at least ten, maybe fifteen rabbits 'fore Christmas; just think; forty dollars, fifty dollars—maybe sixty dollars. Thanks, Mr. Benton, we'll be bringin' you bunches of rabbits in a few days," I said as me and John Clayton headed out the drug store. We were excited, and as we ran back to my house I could just see the sales lady at Samples handing me the red scarf.

We couldn't wait to build the rabbit trap. There were rabbits all around our house and garden, and Flat Creek Swamp was full of them. This was gonna be the easiest money we'd ever made. We rounded up all the stuff we needed where we'd be ready to work on the trap when we got back from the picture show. Daddy honked the horn for us, we ran back around the house, and then we hopped in our car for a trip to El Dorado and the Ritz Theater.

After we got back from the picture show at the Ritz, we took Daddy's saw, hammer, and nails and went to work. It didn't take us but a few hours to finish the trap.

"Okay, John Clayton, let's try it out. Maybe if we put some scraps in it one of our cats would go in and we'd see if it worked."

"Yeah, Richard, if it'll catch a cat then it'll dang sure 'nough catch a rabbit."

Soon we had a trail of meat scraps leading up to the box trap and a big piece right in the back of the trap. I found our big old tomcat, Mouser, sleeping on a bale of hay, picked him up, and set him down in front of the trap where he could smell the meat. Sure enough, Mouser lapped up the scraps, and when he got to the box trap he went right in.

Slam!

Mouser had pushed the stick out of the way, and the trap door had dropped.

"Yes! Yes! Look at that, John Clayton. The box trap works perfectly."

Gosh, were we excited. I'm not kidding; we couldn't wait to set our rabbit trap.

However, Mouser, who's a danged mean kinda crazy cat anyway, wasn't all that happy about being trapped in a small narrow box, and it sounded like a cat going crazy in there. Heck, that box was rocking back and forth as Mouser tried to get out, and when I raised the door to let him out, he came out snarling and scratching. Dang, I never thought I'd run from a cat, but after he took a swipe at John Clayton, I jumped up on a bale of hay to get away from an angry cat. Mouser let out one more snarl and left the barn.

"Haaaah, get outta here, Mouser!" Mouser gave me a hiss and finally trotted out of the barn.

"We've made a perfect rabbit trap, John Clayton. Just think of havin' maybe forty dollars to spend on Christmas presents. Heck, let's set in out behind the barn. I saw two rabbits out there just this mornin'. Get some corn outta the feed barrel, and meet me behind the barn." I picked up the box trap and walked out of the barn.

We put a trail of corn leading up to the box trap and then filled the whole back of the trap with corn.

"That autta do it, Richard. We'll probably have a rabbit in there by mornin'."

We'll probably have caught three or four rabbits by next week, I thought, *and I'll have enough money to go ahead and get the red scarf for Rosalie before somebody else buys it.*

The next morning before my paper route I ran out and sure enough, the trap door was down, and I could hear something scurrying around inside the trap. We'd caught our first rabbit, but since it was still dark I decided to wait until I was through with my paper route to get the rabbit out of the trap. I finished my paper route, and I was so excited as I ran back home and got ready to take the rabbit out of the trap.

"Shoot, that's not a rabbit!" I yelled as I opened the trap door. "It's a big old wharf rat."

Well, sad to say, but after a few days of trying, we found out you couldn't set the box trap anywhere close to the barn or even in the garden. The rats would get in the trap before the rabbits could find it. We gave up after another couple of days.

It was Thursday afternoon, and I still didn't have any Christmas money. I walked in the kitchen and as usual Daddy was twisting the radio dial looking for the Walter Winchell newscast and some news about the war.

"Richard, come here. Walter Winchell is on."

Daddy had finally found KELD on the radio and, our favorite newscaster's voice filled the kitchen with a special war news broadcast.

"*Good evening, Mr. and Mrs. North and South America and all the ships at sea; let's go to press—first in the Philippines; Jap kamikazes attack a twelve-destroyer task force sinking one destroyer—four carriers—*"

"Dang, those sorry Japs!" Daddy yelled as he stood up and started walking around the table.

"Jack, watch your language," said Momma.

Walter Winchell continued, mostly about the kamikazes, but he did mention General Patton, whose 3rd Army had broken through the Siegfried Line and was was roaring across Germany chasing those sorry Germans back to where they came from. Daddy nodded his approval. General Patton is Daddy's favorite General, and according to Daddy, General Patton would have already whipped those sorry Germans, if they'd just let him go.

Friday afternoon after school let out I met John Clayton, Tiny, and Ears in front of Echols Grocery. We were sitting around on the breadbox talking when Homer Ray and a couple of his sorry friends walked up.

Homer Ray is a lot bigger than most of the kids, and he's always giving us trouble. Course he won't hit me no more, but that don't stop him from mouthing and harassing me and hitting my friends.

"Well, if it isn't the whole bunch of dummies all in one pile," laughed Homer Ray.

"Leave us alone, Homer Ray," said Ears, who had started catching most of the bullying from Homer Ray.

Homer Ray ignored Ears and walked up to the breadbox.

"Hey, Ears, do these come off?" He grabbed one of Ears's big ears and gave it a hard yank. Homer Ray's friends just cackled out.

"Oh, dang you, Homer Ray! That hurt!"

"Leave him alone, Homer Ray!" I said.

"Or what? What are you going to do about it, Mr. Skinny?"

I got down from the breadbox and stood between Homer Ray and Ears.

"Go ahead and hit me, Homer Ray, you chicken," I taunted, knowing he wasn't about to hit me.

"Dang you, Richard, one of these days I'll get you so bad you won't believe it," he yelled as he and his worthless friends walked away.

"Chicken! Yellowbelly coward!"

"Dang, Richard, he won't beat up on you none, but if you keep tauntin' him he's gonna take it out on me," said Ears.

"Naw, he's just talk, cause he knows he'll get whipped up on like crazy, if he so much as touches me. Y'all just hang around me and everything will be okay."

We grumbled about sorry Homer Ray for a while, and then we started talking about what we were gonna do on Saturday.

Course the talk about what to do on Saturday was mostly about going to the picture show.

"Richard, I'll bet you can't wait 'til tomorrow. There's a new Tarzan on at the Ritz," said John Clayton. John Clayton knew the Tarzan funny books were my very favorite.

"Yeah, you're durn right I'm gonna see that Tarzan picture show. Heck, I wouldn't miss it for nothin'." John Clayton was right; I couldn't wait for the Saturday picture show at the Ritz, because last week the trailers had been about a new picture show called *Tarzan Desert Mystery*. Course I have every one of the Tarzan funny books, and me and John Clayton play Tarzan when we're deep in the woods swinging from wild grapevines, but tomorrow we'd be seeing the real thing.

"Hey, it's gettin' late; I need to go feed the chickens," I said getting up from the breadbox and starting to walk off. "Meet me at my house at nine-thirty tomorrow," I yelled at John Clayton. "Daddy's drivin' us into El Dorado."

"Okay, see you in the mornin'," said John Clayton.

"Oh, yeah, remember, it's my time to get in free."

"No, it's not, Richard, I let you in last week and the week before that."

"Well, yeah, maybe you did."

Me and John Clayton take turns paying for our ticket, and after the picture show starts the one who paid goes down behind the curtain and opens the outside exit door for the other one. Last year John Clayton got sick and was looking for a place to throw up when he went behind the curtain and found this door that led into the alley.

Well, I do feel a little guilty about sneaking in, but I've noticed old man Slater, the theater manager, just waves by some of his friends and they don't pay. So, heck, why should I?

8

Glasses for Uncle Hugh

Saturday, December 9th, 1944

The next morning Daddy drove us into El Dorado and dropped us off at ten o'clock in front of the Ritz Theater. The Ritz don't open until half past ten so we had a little time to go by the eye doctor's office to buy Uncle Hugh some glasses. We walked down Main Street to the doctor's office, which was on the corner of Main and Washington Street, and there was a lady sitting at a desk and a bunch of people waiting to see the doctor.

That dang John Clayton looked like a scared rabbit when we walked into the doctor's office. He gave me a shove forward, and I stumbled up to the desk where the lady was sitting.

"Uh, uh, ma'am, we're here to buy a friend some glasses. He can't hardly see, and he needs some strong glasses."

"Boys, he has to come in and have his eyes tested. The doctor wouldn't have any idea what strength it would take unless he's tested."

"Well, we live in Norphlet, and we've been a-tryin' to get him here to see y'all, but he's a real old colored man, and he can't make the trip, but I don't think he could buy the glasses even if he made it here. We're gonna buy the glasses for 'em."

"That's real nice of you, boys, but we can't sell you glasses unless the doctor sees your friend."

We were disappointed and about to leave when the doctor came out in the waiting room to get another patient.

"Doctor, these boys have a friend that needs glasses, and he's too feeble to come in and be fitted. Is there any way we can help them?"

"Humm, he can't make it to El Dorado?"

"No sir, he's 'bout a hunnerd years old, and he lives way out in the country," said John Clayton.

The doctor stood there a minute and finally said, "We usually don't do this, but I could give you an eye chart, and you could let your folks give your friend an eye test. I guess we could estimate what strength glasses he needs."

"That'd be great, Doctor. Just tell us how to do the test," I said.

"Boys, the test is simple. Have your friend stand exactly six feet back, and ask him to read the lines on this chart. Make an X on the chart for every line he can read. Do you understand? Have your daddy give him the test."

"Yes sir, we will."

The doctor handed us an eye chart, and we walked back toward the Ritz Theater.

"Shoot, this is so easy. We sure don't need our daddies. Next Saturday we'll come back with the test marked, and we can get Uncle Hugh's some glasses," I said. "Heck, I'll bet they won't cost but a dollar or two."

Boy, the Tarzan picture show was the best I've ever seen, and when Tarzan and the natives dug the pit trap and the bad guys fell into it, every kid in the theater yelled and screamed. Since it was getting close to Christmas most of the trailers were about new Christmas shows, and one of them, the one we really wanted to see, was only gonna show during the week. It was called *The Curse of the Cat People*. Wow, this looked like the kinda picture show we'd really like. Right then me and John Clayton started planning to try and get Daddy to take us back to the Ritz the next Monday night.

Daddy picked us up at one o'clock and on the way back we talked about the picture show, and getting him to take us back for the special Christmas picture show on Monday.

"You know something, John Clayton? When Tarzan caught them bad guys by diggin' a pit and puttin' branches over the hole, it made me think of how we could trap some of them big old coons down in Flat Creek Swamp."

"Whata you mean?"

"What if we dug a hole deep enough to where if a coon fell in it couldn't get out? We'd cover the hole with little twigs and put some chicken scraps on top and, heck, I'll betcha we'd catch a coon."

"Richard, that sounds great. Once a big old coon falls in that hole, we got it."

"Yeah, and every coon that falls in that hole is seven-fifty in Christmas money."

As soon as we got back home we got a shovel, some chicken scraps, and headed for Flat Creek Swamp.

After walking deep into the swamp, we found an open place on a big beech tree mound, started digging, and before long we had a hole about five feet deep and two feet across the top. We made the sides very straight and the bottom larger than the top, where if a coon fell in, it'd have a heck of a tough time climbing out.

I took the chicken scraps out of the sack, and we put them on top of the small sticks and leaves.

"Well, it's ready. Tomorrow after church we'll come down here and check it out."

"Yeah, Richard; this is the smartest thing we've done in a long time."

The next morning we couldn't wait for church to be over. All through Sunday School we whispered back and forth about what we were gonna have in our pit trap. John Clayton came home from church with me, and after Sunday dinner we called Sniffer and headed for the swamp. We ran the whole way to the beech tree rise deep in the swamp. Sunday dinner had been slow, slow, slow, cause the preacher ate with us, and it was getting late by the time we got there. Heck, one of the things I remember the most is that it was getting dark and all the big trees made it look real gloomy. I kinda got a little spooky cause I sure didn't want to be caught deep in the swamp in the dark.

Boy, by the time I got to the pit trap I was gasping for my breath, and I was just so excited I could hardly stand it. I got to the pit trap before John Clayton.

"Something's in the trap!—Look,—there's a hole in the sticks and leaves where it fell through!"

We looked down in the pit, and we could barely make out something dark and furry moving around trying to climb the dirt walls.

"All right! Look at that! Hey, we done caught ourselves a big old coon," I hollered.

"Yeah, but—uh—what now? How are we gonna get the dang coon outta the pit?" John Clayton said.

Well, that was a pretty good question, and I guess we'd been so excited about catching the coon we hadn't even thought about how we were going to get it in a sack to take to Mr. Benton. Heck, I could just look at the white teeth marks on my hand where a big old coon clamped down on my hand last summer when I reached in a hollow log to pull out a rabbit, which weren't no rabbit a-tall but a mean coon; and if I reached down in that hole and grabbed the coon, it was gonna bite the fool out of me. Then I had a pretty good idea.

"Hey, John Clayton; you know somethin'? If we could get a rope around the coon, we could pull it up, drop it in a towsack, and take it over to Mr. Benton's. Heck, we got at least eight dollars right here in this hole, and all we gotta do is get the coon out and in a sack."

"Yeah, Richard, that might work, but who's gonna put the rope around the coon?"

"Heck, John Clayton, we'll just drop a loop over it like those cowboys do cows and pull it up; you hold the sack, and I'll drop it in. This will be so easy you won't believe it. Come on, let's go back to my house and get some heavy cord and a towsack."

We walked and ran back to our barn and found some good strong white cord and a towsack.

"Hurry up, John Clayton, it's gettin' dark, and I'm not about to stay in that spooky swamp after dark." We ran and walked as fast as we could, and in a few minutes we were back at the pit trap ready to lasso the coon.

I got lucky on the first drop of the cord.

"Whoa! Get the sack ready. I've already got the cord 'round its neck, and I'm ready to pull it up." I could feel the coon a-jerking, kicking, and snarling. "I got 'em! I got 'em! Get the sack!"

Sniffer stuck his head down in the mouth of the hole, howling to beat sixty, and John Clayton was on his knees holding the sack out ready to let me drop the coon in it.

"Okay, get ready! Here it comes! And don't ya let it get away!"

Boy, I could feel the coon jerking and snarling as I slowly pulled it up out of the hole. I stopped pulling right before the coon was at the top of the hole, and me, Sniffer, and John Clayton were all on our knees bending over the hole to see the coon.

"Okay, Mr. Coon, come outta that hole!" I stood up and pulled the coon out on the end of the cord.

When I pulled the coon up out of the hole I kinda thought it looked a little different. If fact I was wondering why it had some white fur on its back when John Clayton yelled; "That ain't no coon, Richard! It's a skunk!"

"Nooooooooooo! Look out!" But before we could move the skunk raised its tail and sprayed stuff all over everybody.

"Ahaaaaaaaaa! Ahaaaaaaaaa! Run! Run!" I dropped the skunk on the ground and turned to run.

Clomp! Sniffer, who was right by my side, grabbed the skunk before it hit the ground, and boy, if you thought it sprayed the first time, that weren't nothing to what hit us the second time.

"Ahaaaaaaa! Sniffer! No! No!" I whacked Sniffer on the head to make him turn the skunk loose, which he did, but the skunk sprayed everybody again and Sniffer caught most of it right in his face. Sniffer staggered back howling, pawing his nose and eyes as the skunk trotted off.

"Oh!—Oh, my God! I can't breathe. Ahaaaaaaaaaaaaa! Run for your life!" I wiped my face and eyes, desperately trying to get rid of the stinking smell.

We were jumping around trying to rub the stuff off, and I'm not kidding when I'm telling you it was the worst dang smell you've ever smelt in your whole dang life. Course me and John Clayton were a-yelling and Sniffer was howling to beat sixty, but all the yelling and howling weren't doing no good.

"Ahaaaaaa! Ahaaaaaa! Oh! Oh! Dang! Dang! Dang you, Richard! We smell horrible—This stuff is all over us,—and it's all your stinkin' fault! You stupid idiot!"

"My fault! You thought it was a coon too! You must be blind if you can't tell a skunk from a coon. Why didn't you tell me to drop it back in the hole?"

"You liar! Liar! You sorry liar! What are we gonna do now?"

"Shoot, I don't have a clue. I know one thing for sure, Momma ain't gonna let us come in the house a-smellin' like this."

They weren't nothing to do but slowly walk back to my house with Sniffer, who was stopping to roll in the dirt and paw at his nose every few feet. Wow, I've smelled some bad stuff before, but nothing like what that skunk sprayed us with.

We walked up to our back door, and I called out to Daddy.

Daddy walked out and before he even got near us he said, "What's wrong? What's that I smell?"

"Uh, well, Daddy, we happened to get too close to a skunk."

Daddy started to smile as he stood there in the door. He walked down the steps to check us out, but before the door slammed shut Sniffer went running in the kitchen.

I could hear Momma screaming at Sniffer all the way out in the back yard. Sniffer burst back through the door with Momma swinging a broom.

"What in the world has that dog rolled in now? My kitchen smells horrible!"

Then Momma saw us standing there with our heads up trying not to smell the skunk stuff that was all over our clothes.

"What? What in the world have you boys been into now?"

"Skunk got us, Momma."

"Skunk got you? What in the world were you doing gettin' close enough to a skunk to get sprayed?"

"Uh, well, Momma, we had this trap just like Tarzan, and—"

"Oh, my gosh, well, strip off your clothes. You can't come in this house smellin' like that."

"What? What?" said John Clayton, who dang sure didn't want to take off his clothes in front of Momma.

"I'll go get a bar of Lava soap, and you boys can stand out here in the back yard and bathe while your daddy holds the garden hose on you. Now, get out of those clothes, and put them in the wash pot. Jack, fill the pot with water and boil those clothes for about thirty minutes, and put about a quarter cup of Pine-Sol in with them."

Momma was all business, and even though it was about thirty-five degrees and getting dark, I started undressing.

I got everything off, and Daddy picked up our clothes with a stick and dropped them in the wash pot. He started a fire with pine kindling and threw everything I had on, including my shoes, in the pot.

"Okay, boys; Richard, you're first, take this bar of soap and wash while I hold this hose over you." Daddy turned the hose on, I turned around, and a full stream of cold water hit me right in the middle of my back. When the first drop hit my bare skin, I jumped three feet high.

"Ahaaaaaa, Daddy! Stop! Stop! It's too cold! I'm freezin' to death!"

"Richard, stop whinin' and start scrubbin' with that bar of soap."

So, for the next ten minutes I spent the most miserable time of my life standing in the back yard in the dark with cold water cascading over me, scrubbing like crazy, while John Clayton stood there grinning like a possum.

"You're not finished, Richard. Wash your hair."

"Oh, Daddy, it's too cold. Ahaaaaa!" I yelled as Daddy stuck the hose in my hair.

John Clayton laughed out loud as I jumped around trying to dodge the stream of cold water.

Finally I was through, and Momma handed me a towel. I was shaking so badly I could hardly hold the towel, but anything was better than having that cold water from a hose splashing on my back.

When I grabbed the towel, I smiled for the first time, thinking about John Clayton having to pull off his underwear in front of Momma. *When that cold water hits him he's gonna go crazy,* I thought. I was really gonna enjoy watch him yell and hop around.

Well, John Clayton didn't want to take off his underwear, but he leaned over and smelled it and then shaking his head he turned away from Momma and took it off.

"Ahaaaaaaa! Ahaaaaaa!" More screaming about the cold water from John Clayton and finally we were finished, and with a warm towel wrapped around us we huddled back on my bed while Momma hunted up some extra clothes. In a few minutes Momma stuck her head in the door and announced we were gonna hafta do without jackets until those came out of the wash pot and dried.

"Boys," Momma said, "when you get those clothes on go out and dip out the clothes from the wash pot and hang them on the clothesline. It's going to take 'til tomorrow to dry in this weather."

We walked out, took a stick, and forked out our clothes. After we had hung them on the clothesline we started back for the house only to be greeted by Sniffer.

"Ahaa, that dang dog still stinks," I said.

"Richard, here, take this soap and wash that dog." It was Daddy standing there on the steps with the of Lava soap in his hand.

"Aw, Daddy, we're gonna get all stinky again."

"Richard, that dog deserves to be clean, and since you're the one that caused him to get skunk musk on him, you wash him."

Well, me and John Clayton washed a most unwilling dog, and finally we finished and ran inside to huddle by a roaring fireplace.

"Richard, I swear on a stack of Bibles ten feet tall, if you get us into anything else like that I'm gonna pound you good," mumbled John Clayton as we sat in front of the fireplace.

"Baloney, it was as much your fault as mine."

Well, we complained a bunch about the skunk, but finally we started laughing about it, and after we told the story several times we were almost bragging about catching that skunk.

I went to bed that night thinking about nearly having some Christmas money. *Dang, I thought, if it had just been a coon.* But then I shook my head as I thought about resetting the trap. *No, I ain't 'bout to catch 'nother skunk if I never get no Christmas money.*

9

The Eye Test

Sunday, December 10th, 1944

That night as I lay in my bed I could still smell a hint of skunk, and I knew I'd hafta take several more baths to get all the stuff out of my hair.

Well, I thought, *'nother plan for Christmas money that didn't work.* Before I went to sleep I daydreamed about giving Rosalie the red scarf and having her give me a great big hug. *Not gonna happen,* I thought as I drifted off to sleep.

Sunday rolled around and the weather warmed up a bunch. You didn't even need a long-sleeve shirt, and in place of the cold north wind a warm southeast wind off the Gulf of Mexico brought the temperature up past seventy degrees. We headed to Uncle Hugh's house with our eye chart.

"Uncle Hugh! Uncle Hugh! It's Richard and John Clayton," we yelled from the front steps.

Uncle Hugh opened the door, and we walked in with me waving the eye chart.

"Uncle Hugh, we're gonna give you an eye test today, and tomorrow, if Daddy lets us go to the picture show, we'll get you some glasses. Stand back against the wall. Say, John Clayton, how far is six feet?"

"Boys, do y'all know what you is a-doin'?"

"Sure, this is so easy. All you hafta do is read these lines on this eye chart."

We finally figured out the six feet, and started the test.

"Okay, Uncle Hugh, start readin' any line you can."

"Richard, I can't read none of 'um."

"What?"

"Naw, everything is so dark, I can't make out nothin'."

John Clayton piped up. "Heck, Richard, with only an old coal oil lamp in here, it's so dim I can barely read the chart. We need to get on the porch."

He was right, and after moving outside, Uncle Hugh read a couple of the biggest lines, but that was it. I ain't no eye doctor, but I knew he needed real strong glasses.

Gosh, it was really hard to convince Daddy to let us go to the picture show again that next Monday, but after we whined that all our friends were going, he finally agreed to take us. Daddy left us off at four, and since the picture show didn't start 'til five, we had plenty of time to go to the eye doctor's office.

We had to wait a long time in the waiting room. Finally, the doctor came out and talked to us.

"Well, boys, did y'all get your friend to take the eye test?"

"Yes, sir, here it is," and I handed it to the eye doctor.

"Hmmm, well, he's going to need very strong reading glasses, but I think we have a pair here in the office."

He walked back to behind the desk and pulled out several drawers until he found the pair he was looking for.

"Yes, these will do. Okay, boys, tell your friend if these glasses are too strong and everything is blurred, bring them back, and we'll exchange them. Remember, these are reading glasses."

"Yes, sir, and thank you so much for helpin' us." I looked over at John Clayton. "Gimme your two dollars."

"Glad you came by, boys. Maude, charge these boys just fifteen dollars for these glasses, since I didn't have to make an examination."

I looked at John Clayton as he looked at me.

"Fifteen dollars? Uh, uh, sir, we didn't think it would be anything near that much. We have four and a half. Could we charge the rest and pay you over the next few weeks?"

"Son, I'd like to help you, but we have a hard and fast rule. We don't let our glasses leave here unless they're paid for in full.

We'll stick them in the desk, and when y'all get your money together, stop back in and pick 'um up."

We left the doctor's office feeling kinda bad about not having money to buy the glasses. Heck, we didn't even have enough money for Christmas presents so there weren't no way on God's green earth to come up with fifteen dollars.

"Richard, you can forget 'bout helpin' Uncle Hugh get new glasses, and Uncle Hugh sure can't buy 'um. He ain't got 'nough money to buy groceries."

"Yeah, you're right."

Well, we sure felt bad about not being able to pay for Uncle Hugh's glasses, but later when we told Uncle Hugh, he laughed, said not to worry, he was getting along fine, and he thanked us for trying.

We were back at the Ritz before five, and as usual John Clayton was whining about being cold.

"Richard, you told me to wear a short-sleeve shirt, and now I'm freezin' to death."

"Heck, it must have gotten colder since I ran the paper route. It's sure not my fault. Whata you expect me to do control the weather, or make you smart enough to wear a long sleeve shirt?"

John Clayton just mumbled something and started complaining about the ticket window not being open when worthless Homer Ray and a couple of his sorry friends walked up.

"Well, if isn't the dumb, dumb twins," he sneered.

"Get lost, Homer Ray," I yelled.

"Dang, open that ticket window. I'm freezin' to death," John Clayton said as he rapped on the window.

"You're probably gonna be colder in the theater," said Homer Ray as he walked off grinnin' a big *I know somethin' you don't* grin.

"What did he mean by that?" said John Clayton.

"Shoot, I don't have a clue. Maybe they're not gonna have the heat on."

"How in the heck would Homer Ray know the heat wasn't gonna be on?"

"Hey, come on; the ticket window's opened."

I didn't think any more about Homer Ray's little comments until later. John Clayton bought a ticket, and Ears, Tiny, and I went around to the exit door and snuck in. We walked down to the front row of the theater and sat in our usual seats. The picture show had started and the lights were down low where you couldn't see anything, when something sailed over the top of the seats behind us and hit us.

"Ahaaaaa! Ahaaaaaa! I'm wet!" I jumped up and looked around to see who threw the three water balloons at us. Our whole group of friends were soaking wet. The kids right behind us said the water balloons came from back of them, and as I looked back through the dim light I could make out the grinning face of that worthless Homer Ray.

"Homer Ray, I'm tellin' Mr. Slater! He's gonna whip your sorry hide!"

"For what?" Homer Ray yelled back.

"You know what! Dang you!"

"Hey, what in the heck is all that yellin' 'bout?"

It was Mr. Slater, the theater manager.

"Mr. Slater, Homer Ray threw water balloons at us, and we're all wet."

"I did not, Mr. Slater," Homer Ray protested.

Mr. Slater started taking off his belt, and Homer Ray began to yell, beg, and say he didn't do it. I thought Mr. Salter was gonna grab him up and beat the fool out of him, and then I saw Mr. Slater look at me and John Clayton, recognize us, and make a little smile.

"Huh, you Norphlet boys got a little of your own medicine." He put his belt back on and walked back up the aisle.

Well, maybe we did have something to do with some of the stuff that had happened at the Ritz—like letting a big old possum go right in the middle of a theater full of little kids—but he couldn't prove nothing.

We were cold and wet for almost the entire picture show. Finally, when the show was about over, we dried out.

"Just you wait, John Clayton. That's the last straw. I'm gonna teach that sorry Homer Ray a lesson he won't forget for the rest of his worthless life."

"I hope you hurry up and do somethin'. He's makin' life miserable for us."

"I've got a plan for Homer Ray, but we need to be in school."

10

Stopping the Bully

Tuesday, December 12th, 1944

Dang, I sure hated to go to school that next day, but there wasn't no choice, so after finishing my chores and having break-fast, I plodded down the road to school.

John Clayton was waiting for me when I walked on the play-ground.

"Richard, we gotta do somethin' 'bout Homer Ray. He knows you pointed him out to old man Slater yesterday, and he can't pick on you no more, so he's takin' it out on everybody that runs around with you. Heck, he's got Ears almost cryin' over there, and he's slapped me across the back of my head so hard I seen stars."

"Dang that sorry son-of-a-gun, he's not gonna get away with that." I started for Homer Ray, who had Ears cornered against the building and was shoving him back into the brick wall every time Ears tried to get away.

"Ahaaa, oh, don't Homer Ray. Please stop," said Ears who was on the verge of crying.

I shook my head and walked straight over to where they were scuffling. *Dang, I know this is gonna hurt,* I thought, *but it's worth it.*

It was time to put my plan into action.

"Hey, Mr. Jerk!" I stepped between Homer Ray and Ears and shoved Homer Ray back. "Why don't you hit me, you big-mouth bully? Or maybe you've got a yellow streak a foot wide runnin' up your slimy back."

"Get outta here, Richard. Stay outta this or you'll regret it," he said, trying to ignore me.

Homer Ray was turning red in the face as he tried to shove me away, but I wasn't having any of that. I felt John Clayton pull on my arm, trying to get me to stop, but I was just getting started.

"Hey, you big dumb ugly monkey, don't push me!" I shoved him again and got right up in his face.

"Get away from me, Richard, or I'll break your skinny neck!"

"Ha! You gutless, whiny weenie! Make me! Make me!" I screamed right in his face as I gave him a big shove, and jabbed him in the stomach real hard with my thumb and twisted it.

"Oh! Dang you, Richard!"

"Chicken! Chicken! Chicken!" I yelled right in his face as my friends watched, not believing what I was doing.

"Richard! Don't!" John Clayton yelled just as Homer Ray drew back to swing.

Homer Ray's fist caught me right in the mouth, and I staggered back with blood running down my chin from a busted lip.

"Ahaaaa, oh, my mouth!" I moaned as I turned and started to walk away, but before I left Homer Ray, I smiled back at him and said, "Homer Ray, you're gonna regret that swing for a long, long time." He had done exactly what I thought he'd do, and now he was in more trouble than he could ever imagine.

Homer Ray stood there for a minute and then a look of shock came over his face, as he realized what he'd just done.

"Wait a minute, Richard! You made me hit you. It was your fault. You hit me first. Wait, Richard—"

I kept walking 'til I was in the classroom. He tried to talk with me several times during the day, but I didn't pay no attention to him. He was in a bunch of trouble, and he sure as heck knew it.

As soon as I got home I walked out to the barn where Daddy was fixing a fence between the barn and the chicken yard, and I told him how Homer Ray had hit me in the face for no reason at all, and I showed him my busted lip. Boy, was Daddy mad.

"He's bullying you again?" said Daddy, who had laid his hammer down and was getting madder by the minute.

"Yeah, Daddy, he just reared back and slugged me for no reason a-tall. I wasn't doing nothin', and he said he was gonna beat up on me for the rest of the school year."

"You didn't do anything, and he hit you; for no reason at all?"

"That's right, Daddy, and he said tomorrow he was gonna beat the sense outta me, unless I brought him a quarter."

"What? He's trying to make you pay him money to quit bullying you?"

"Yes, sir, just ask John Clayton. He heard him say it."

"By God! I warned Fred!"

"Oh, yeah, Daddy, Homer Ray said his daddy weren't 'fraid of you. Homer Ray said Mr. Parks could whip up on you, if he wanted to."

"What?"

"Yeah, Daddy, that's what he said."

"We'll see about that."

I knew all that stuff wasn't exactly the truth, but heck, as sorry as Homer Ray is, he probably would come up with something like that sooner or later, and I knew John Clayton would back up my story, if it had to do with worthless Homer Ray. Heck, sometimes little white lies will make things right. I'll tell you one thing; I might feel bad about sneaking in the Ritz and even getting one of old man Odom's watermelons last summer, but I dang sure didn't worry a whit about stretching the truth to get stupid Homer Ray whipped up on. Man oh man, I could hardly wait.

"Whip me? That sorry son-of-a-gun will regret the day he said that!" Daddy picked up the hammer, chunked it across the chicken yard, and headed for the car. Boy, I don't think I've ever seen my red-headed daddy that mad.

"Get in the car, Richard! We're going to have a little talk with Homer Ray's dad. I told him if Homer Ray hit you again, he was gonna deal with me, and by God, when I get through with him, Homer Ray won't ever even think about bullying you!"

We jumped in the car, tires squealed, and we roared down the road. In a few minutes we pulled up to the Parks house. Their house is a small, white frame house with a long front porch. It's a block south of Main Street in a rundown section of town.

Our car came to a sliding stop in front of their house, and Daddy hopped out of the car and walked up to the front porch steps.

"Fred! Fred Parks! Come out here! We need to talk!" Daddy paced back and forth in front of the front porch mumbling something.

It wasn't but a few seconds until skinny little Fred Parks stepped out on the front porch.

"Fred, didn't I tell you to keep that kid of yours from beating up on Richard?" Daddy yelled, pointing his finger at a cowed Mr. Parks. "And what's that talk about whippin' me?"

"Huh?"

"You heard me!"

"Now, Jack, calm down; Homer Ray told me Richard done started the fight. He said Richard brought it on hisself. You need to tend to Richard, for startin' somethin'."

It really didn't matter a whit what Mr. Parks told Daddy, cause Daddy, a hot-tempered redhead, was so mad nothing Mr. Parks could have said would have stopped him. When I saw Daddy start shaking his head, I knew Mr. Parks was about to be in deep trouble.

"Let me refresh your memory, you sorry son-of-a-gun!" He reached up, grabbed Mr. Parks by the front his overalls, and yanked him off the porch, knocking Mr. Parks's ever-present cigarette out of his mouth. Daddy never turned loose of Mr. Parks's overalls as he pounded him with his free hand.

It wasn't much of a fight at all. Mr. Parks tried to fend off a few blows, but his skinny hands and arms didn't stop Daddy's fists.

"Oh! Oh! Ahaaa! Please stop, Jack. It won't happen again, I promise!"

Daddy still had a head of steam, and poor Mr. Parks caught another half dozen blows from Daddy's big right hand, before Daddy dropped the bloodied, battered Mr. Parks, who hit the ground like a sack of potatoes. Mr. Parks sat there wiping the blood off his mouth, swearing to Daddy that he'd beat the life out of Homer Ray, if he ever touched me again. I could see Homer Ray standing behind the screen door shaking like a wet cat, and I gave him a smile and a little wave. When we drove off Mr. Parks had already cut a whopping big switch and was going for Homer Ray. I just wished I could've watched Homer Ray get the snot beat out of him.

The next day at school Homer Ray drug in like a whipped-up dog. No more bullying, but he whispered to me when we were alone, "Richard, if it's the last thing I ever do, I'm gonna get you for that."

"Ha, go ahead, hit me again, Mr. Double Jerk," I sneered, "and I'll have you whipped like a yard dog. And listen to me," I whispered as I got up real close to him, "if you pick on any of my friends, I'll make up some story to tell my daddy, and he'll be back over to beat the fool outta your daddy again, and then you'll get whipped like you ain't never been whipped. You understand; Mr. Jerk? Now get your sorry butt away from me." I put my hand right in his face and shoved him back.

"You—you—one of these days, I'll get you so bad!"

Then Homer Ray walked away, and I knew that was gonna be the end of our problems with him—at least for a while.

I'll say one thing; the standing-up to Homer Ray had Rosalie taking notice.

Rosalie walked by right after I called Homer Ray a double jerk, and she stopped to talk with me. Rosalie was glad somebody had finally gotten the best of Homer Ray, and thought it was a brave thing to make him hit me so his daddy would whip the dickens out of him. Rosalie stayed and talked with me until the bell rang, kidding and laughing about Homer Ray and school.

While we were talking Rosalie pulled her jacket up, trying to keep the wind off her neck. *The red scarf,* I thought. *She'll love it. I've got to buy it if it's the last thing I ever do.*

11

Wing and Peg

Wednesday, December 13th, 1944

School let out at half past three, but heck, I never go straight home. I headed downtown with John Clayton, and we met Ears and Tiny at the breadbox. I had some chores to do when I got home, but as long as I did them before supper it was okay. Ears was really happy.

"Shoot, Richard, I don't know what the heck you did to Homer Ray, but he's just plain stopped bullyin' everybody. Heck, I walked right by 'em today, and he didn't touch me."

"Oh, Ears, I just put the fear of God in him."

"Ha! I know better than that," hooted John Clayton. "Richard's daddy beat the fool outta Mr. Parks, and I heard Mr. Parks nearly whipped Homer Ray to death."

"Well, yeah, but I took a real hit in the mouth. That autta count for something," I said.

"Heck, I don't care who or what, I'm just glad he stopped," said Ears.

We were yakking away when; "Hey, boys, y'all stayin' outta trouble?"

Wing, the town marshal, had walked up to the breadbox and as usual, he was teasing us. Wing's the brother of Peg Ellenberger, the owner of the local pool hall, and his nickname is Wing cause he ain't got but one arm, but shoot, Wing can swing his blackjack with his one arm and take people out left and right. Daddy told me Wing lost his arm when he was a little boy playing around some machinery at a cotton gin. When Wing applied for the job of town marshal several people wondered if he could handle things with only one arm. They found out real quick that Wing was able to handle any of the fights and problems around Norphlet. Wing's a good friend and he's always coming by the breadbox to talk with us.

Everybody really likes Wing. He's a whole lot better than Constable Curly Sawyer, the old sot. Wing's a tall, thin man who stands as straight as a ramrod, and he always wears a big cowboy hat like some old Western marshal. Course everyone in town knows Wing's reputation with a blackjack. I ain't never seen Wing when he wasn't twirling his blackjack around.

"Shoot, Wing, we ain't never in trouble, but some people blame us for stuff other kids do," said Tiny.

"Oh, really?" questioned Wing. "What about Henry Odom's watermelon patch last summer?"

As soon as Wing mentioned old man Odom's watermelon patch, I felt my face start to turn red. Me and Ears had raided it last summer and carried off his prize seventy-pound, possible world-record, watermelon, but he couldn't prove nothing, since we had feedsacks over our heads. John Clayton laughed, but Ears looked as guilty as sin.

"Uh, well, I heard whoever got in that melon patch had feed-sacks over their heads," I said.

"Oh, boys, don't y'all get all uptight, I'm just foolin' 'round with y'all. Heck, if I was your age, I woulda been right there with you. By the way, what did y'all do with the big watermelon?"

"Uh, well, we—" Ears was about to blab the whole dang thing.

I gave him a *no, no* shake of the head, and I cut my hand across my throat as I yelled, "Wing, I heard them Parnell brothers got that melon."

Wing laughed as he walked off.

"Almost got ya. Didn't I?" he hollered back.

As soon as he was around the corner, I grabbed Ears. "Dang you, Ears! Wing's the law, and I don't care what he says 'bout what he would or wouldn't do. Don't you remember, old man Odom put out a twenty-five dollar reward if them watermelon thieves was 'rrested. Shoot, Wing woulda had us nailed if you'd opened your stupid mouth."

"Oh, heck, Richard, Wing's not gonna turn us in."

"Oh, yes he would, Ears. He fined Peg for takin' a beer out on the sidewalk, and Peg's his brother."

Peg gets his nickname from his wooden peg-leg which makes him look like some old pirate wearing old beat-up overalls. Daddy is one of Peg's best customers, and I know Peg real well. He's a good friend, and I can stop by and tell him stuff and get his advice on all kinda things.

"Hey, y'all, Daddy said Wing had to break up a fight last night at Peg's Place. Let's go down and ask Peg about it," I said. Everybody was curious about Wing breaking up a fight, cause he always uses the blackjack he twirls around. If Wing breaks up a fight it usually means somebody got blackjacked. Gosh, he can hit a man three or four times before you can blink.

We rounded the corner, and there was Peg sweeping out some trash. A broken chair was on the sidewalk.

"Good gosh, Peg, what in the world happened?" said John Clayton.

"Well, boys, that bunch of worthless roughnecks that works on Crotty's drillin' rig was in here raisin' a ruckus; you know, drinkin' like a bunch of fish, yellin' and irritatin' everybody, until old crusty Bobo Morrison, who was playin' dominos, finally had 'nough, and he told 'um to hold it down. Heck, that's all he said. Well, that big old tall roughneck, you know, the one they call Big Six, came over and grabbed old skinny Bobo by the front of his overalls, lifted him right out of his domino chair, and started to shake him like a rag doll. I ran out in the street and hollered for Wing, cause I knowed we's gonna have a fight in just 'bout thirty seconds. Old Bobo's a scrawny old man, but he's tough as a boot, and he don't fight fair neither.

"Wing was down on the corner by Hill Kennedy's Grocery, and he started coming my way as I ran back in the pool hall in time to see Bobo grab Big Six by the throat with both hands and squeeze. Dang, old Bobo was doing some good too, and that sorry roughneck couldn't break his hold. Boy, in about ten seconds Big Six went to his knees squealin' like a stuck hog, and that woulda been all of it, if one of them other roughnecks hadn't walked over and kicked old Bobo right in the ribs. Bobo turned loose of Big Six's throat, sprawled out in the floor, and the guy that kicked him was fixin' to stomp Bobo when Wing came through the door. Heck, Wing walked up like he was just comin' in for a beer and *whap, whap,* he sent Big Six and that other roughneck to the floor with that blackjack of his, and Big Six fell on one of my chairs and broke it all to pieces."

"Gosh, Peg, what did the third roughneck do?"

"Heck, Richard, he acted like he was just watchin' and went back to drinkin' beer. He sure didn't want to be introduced to Wing's blackjack. Wing helped Bobo up and kicked Big Six right in the ribs as he was tryin' to get up. With the work Bobo did on his throat and the lump on his head from Wing's blackjack, Big Six could barely make it out the door. The other one crawled out through the door with Wing right behind him givin' him a kick every now and then. But let me tell you somethin', boys. They's a bad bunch. Later, when the one that was left had 'nother couple of beers, I overheard him talkin' about gettin' Bubba and Wing. 'Teach those hicks a lesson,' that's what he said. I told Wing to watch out, but he just laughed and twirled that blackjack around."

We walked back to the breadbox laughing about Wing cleaning house with his blackjack and sat around for another thirty minutes until Ears and Tiny decided to go home.

12

The Big Snow and the Return
of the Chicken-Killing Coon

Thursday, December 14th, 1944

About a week before Christmas it got a way bunch colder, and that made the paper route the sorriest job any kid in the whole wide world could ever have. One of them super-duper charged cold fronts from way up north roared into south Arkansas and dropped the temperature down to below ten degrees. It was the coldest weather we've had in the last ten years, and my gosh; I can't stand cold weather.

Late last fall we stopped by Uncle Hugh's cabin, and he told us that all the signs said it was gonna be a cold winter. Well, Uncle Hugh was durn sure right about the winter being bad. That Saturday morning I headed out to deliver papers wearing everything I owned. I had on two pair of socks, my heavy jacket, the wool cap that Grandmother knitted pulled down over my ears, and a pair of Daddy's old work gloves.

I waddled into the newsstand dang near frozen.

"Doc, it's too cold to deliver papers." But Doc just ignored me and threw me the bale of papers to roll. I sat there and mumbled about freezing to death as I rolled the papers. The papers were thin and light, and I thought about running the route to keep warm, but then, looking out the door at the streetlight, I saw something, and then a whole bunch more stuff coming down.

"Doc, it's snowin'!" I opened the door and ran out in the street.

"Huh, well, it won't 'mount to much. Never does down here in south Arkansas." He wheeled over to the door to get a good look. Doc clamped down on that old cigarette holder, and it stood up like some weather vane as he pronounced this to be just a "small, won't amount to nothing" flurry.

Boy, that snow put me in a good mood now. Heck, the idea of walking my paper route with it snowing was enough to send me out in the most miserable weather I'd ever seen. Doc was sure wrong about the snow not amounting to nothing. It spit snow until about mid-day, then it picked up and peppered little pieces of ice for most of the afternoon covering the ground with a mixture of snow and sleet. Before I went to bed I walked out on the front porch and checked the snow one more time.

"Yeah," I mumbled to myself, "no school tomorrow." I nodded my head in satisfaction as I looked out over a white yard, an ice-coated road out front, and a regular blizzard of falling sleet. Heck, Norphlet lets school out when it even threatens to snow, so this was a cinch, and sure enough, overnight the sleet changed to snow—and not only snow, but great big flakes—and it was coming down like crazy when I got up. I couldn't wait to get downtown to deliver papers in the snow. I walked the mile into Norphlet taking my time as I made snowballs and threw them at stop signs. I was getting close to the newsstand when I noticed there were no lights on in the City Café, and then I could see the newsstand. It was dark as pitch. As I stood there in front of the newsstand for a few minutes, I figured it out. An old pickup truck came by sliding all over the road and, as it tried to turn the corner at Hill Kennedy's Grocery, it slid all the way across the road into the ditch.

Yep, I thought, Doc's not 'bout to get out and try to drive in this weather, and even if he did, I wouldn't have no papers to deliver. I yelled "Yes!" as loud as I could. Now, I would only have to feed the mules and chickens, and I'd have the whole day off. Heck, I couldn't wait to call John Clayton and get him to come over. We'd track some rabbits, or shoot; we might just make a world record snowman.

Momma was already up fixing breakfast when I ran back in the house.

"Momma, everything is shut down. Doc didn't make it to the newsstand, and I saw a truck run off in the ditch. I'll bet you school's gonna let out Monday."

"Richard, you may be right, but it's about stopped snowing. It may melt after a while."

"Momma, do you know how cold it is out there? Yesterday, it got down to ten degrees, and it's not no warmer—"

"Richard!"

Dang, I thought. *'Nother grammar lesson.* But I said, "Yes ma'am?"

"No warmer?"

"Uh, sorry, Momma; any warmer."

Momma nodded her head and I continued; "Shoot, it's gonna have to warm up fast to melt all that snow."

"Well, Richard, you may be right, but cold, snow, or whatever, the chickens and mules still have to be fed. Hurry up; the biscuits are about ready to come out of the oven."

I nodded, pulled my cap down over my ears, and headed out to feed the chickens. As I got closer to the chicken yard, even in the early morning light, I could see something was bad wrong; chickens were a-running everywhere, cackling to high heaven. It was barely morning and cold as heck. I thought I'd have to put their feed inside, but no, they were all out of the chicken house running around in the snow going crazy. I ain't never seen nothing like it.

"What in the world?" I muttered. I stood there and looked out over the snow-covered chicken yard. Then I saw it; chicken feathers on top of the snow near the door to the pen, and as I ran closer, blood! Something had come into our chicken house and killed one of our chickens. The trail of blood and feathers led to the fence where whatever it was had jumped over, still carrying the chicken. I looked at the tracks carefully as I followed them out across our garden. Every few feet there were a few feathers and some drops of blood. The tracks were a little different and a whole lot bigger than the possum tracks I was used to seeing in the mud. These couldn't be possum tracks, they were too big.

Heck, it's that big old chicken-killin' coon again, come up from the swamp and got one of our chickens.

I went in and told Momma all about the coon getting in our chicken house and carrying off a chicken while she finished up breakfast. She pulled out a pan of big cat-head biscuits from the oven and sat them on the table. Wow, the wonderful baked-bread smell of those biscuits filled the room, and I couldn't wait to tie into them. The biscuits recipe is from my Grandmother Noggle who lives up in Oklahoma. Well, I lathered on a bunch of home-made butter, put some mayhaw jelly on the biscuits, finished off two, and I'd just started on a couple of eggs and some bacon when Daddy opened the door. He'd been working graveyards at the refinery, and he looked frozen.

"Dang! I nearly froze to death—"

"Jack! Watch your language."

"Oh, God! I'm so dang cold—"

"Jack!"

"Sue, I couldn't get the car out of the parkin' lot, and I had to walk home. I'm so dang cold. Where's the coffee?"

Momma let Daddy go on the *dang* this time, since he did look miserable.

Daddy grabbed the cup of coffee from Momma and sat down beside me.

"Daddy, guess what?"

"I don't know, Richard? What?"

"That big old coon got in the chicken house again last night and killed a chicken. There's blood and feathers all over the chicken yard, and it carried the chicken off; jumped right over the fence."

"Really? Is that right?"

"Yes, sir, and it left some good tracks in the snow. Why don't we go track it down after breakfast? You can take the shotgun and shoot the coon when we find it."

Daddy glanced out the window and shook his head.

"Richard, I wouldn't go out there and track a coon down for

a hundred dollars. I worked all night out in this mess, and I nearly froze to death walkin' from the refinery."

"Well, Daddy, can me and John Clayton take Sniffer and track the coon down? Remember last year when Sniffer caught that coon in the garden? Heck, Sniffer can sure whip any old coon even this big 'un, especially if we're there to help."

"Richard, I've been workin' all night loadin' tank cars with asphalt, and I can't wait to hit the bed. If you and John Clayton want to wander around in that dang swamp and freeze to death, go right ahead, but don't wake me up when you come back in."

I smiled as Daddy went over to the stove to get a second cup of coffee. Momma looked a little concerned, but Daddy just waved his hand at her and said, "Sue, they won't stay out there thirty minutes."

Momma nodded and went back to washing dishes while I headed for the telephone to call John Clayton.

"John Clayton, get over here as fast as you can. That big old coon was in our chicken house last night, and he killed a chicken leavin' a trail of blood, feathers, and tracks. Shoot, we can track it down, and between you, me, and Sniffer, we can catch it. A coon that big is at least a seven-fifty coon and maybe even ten dollars after we sell the meat—Yeah—Come on, I'll get the stuff ready."

I hung up the telephone and stood there a minute after I said "ten dollars." Yes, I thought; *the red scarf probably costs ten dollars. Mr. Coon, you're gonna buy Rosalie that red scarf—you just don't know it yet.*

John Clayton was at my house in fifteen minutes, and we bundled up as best we could. Boy, were we excited.

13

The Hunt for the Big Chicken-Killing Coon

Friday, December 15th, 1944

We took our slingshots, a towsack to put the coon in, and found some sticks we could use as clubs to help Sniffer whip the coon. Sniffer was already waiting in the yard circling around letting out one of them long, lonesome, hound howls about every five seconds. Me and John Clayton ran for the chicken yard with Sniffer right behind us. Gosh, I don't think I've ever been that excited.

"Here, Sniffer! Here! Here! Come on! Eyeeee! Git 'em! Git 'em!" I yelled as we opened the chicken yard gate. Sniffer, who has been banned from the chicken yard for sucking eggs, didn't want to go in at first, but when I ran over to the tracks and blood, clapping my hands, he roared right in.

Hooooooo! Hoooooooooo! Hooooooo!

"Eaaaa! Yaaaa! Go git 'em, Sniffer!" I yelled as Sniffer headed out across the field with us running and yelling behind him. Sure enough, the dang chicken-killing coon was heading straight for Flat Creek Swamp. The hunt for the chicken-killing coon was on!

We took off into the woods right in the back of our farm running to keep up with Sniffer, who was howling to beat sixty. The snow was at least ten inches deep, and it immediately filled our low-cut shoes, but with all the excitement we didn't pay no 'ttention to that.

"Come on, John Clayton, Sniffer's gettin' too far ahead!" I stomped and ran through the deep snow following a howling hound who was barely in sight.

We stopped to catch our breath after we got a little further into the swamp, and Sniffer, who we could see through the pin oak flat, was circling around a big thicket of blackberry bushes.

"Dang, Richard, my feet are frozen. Are you sure this is a good idea?"

About that time Sniffer started going dog crazy, howling and running round that blackberry patch.

"Hurry, John Clayton, Sniffer's got 'em hemmed in!" We ran through the snow toward the blackberry patch, and in a few minutes we'd made it to where Sniffer was running around the thick mass of bushes just out of his dog mind. As we got closer, I saw a scattering of chicken feathers, and there it was; our dead chicken, or at least part of it. Evidently, the coon stopped to eat the chicken and then went into the blackberry patch. Sniffer was hanging back, and we started egging him on.

"Git 'em Sniffer! Eeeeee! Yaaaaaaa! Sic 'em! Sic 'em!" I clapped my hands and started pulling the blackberry vines aside, where we could go into the patch. Sniffer got all worked up again and plunged in right ahead of us, and then, when Sniffer was out of sight, in the densest part of the blackberry patch, he picked up his howling like some wild crazy dog, barking little short howls and growling like he was trying to attack.

"Sniffer sees the coon! Come on! We gotta get in there and help 'em! That big coon whipped him last time." We struggled and pushed deeper into the blackberry patch, getting all tangled up and cut from the stickers on the blackberry bushes, when all of a sudden, a snarl, a howl of pain from Sniffer, and the dangdest fight you ever heard started with Sniffer and the coon. They were right in front of us in the middle of some thick bushes, and after about ten seconds it sounded like Sniffer was getting killed.

"Come on, John Clayton; hurry!"

We pushed deeper into the blackberry patch with blackberry vines wrapped around our legs until we were almost to the fight. Then, after another huge snarl from the coon and a frantic yelp from Sniffer, the coon bolted out the other side of the patch with Sniffer right behind it.

"Eeeeeee! Yahaaaaaaa! Git 'em, Sniffer! Git 'em!" The chase started up again. We finally made it out of the other side of the patch, scratched up something terrible, and started after Sniffer and the coon, who by now were about a hundred yards ahead of us.

"Uh, dang, Richard,—that sounded like one big coon,—and I caught a glimpse of it 'fore it got back in the woods—It looked as big as Sniffer," said John Clayton who was hanging his head, panting like he was dying. Heck, I could tell he was about ready to quit, but I sure wasn't.

"Yeah, probably a dang world-record coon! Think 'bout it, John Clayton; a world record, a world-record coon!" Wow, I was running through the woods just thinking about bringing that coon back home and how everybody was gonna be so excited.

I stopped running to catch my breath and I looked over at John Clayton and said, "Shoot, Daddy's not gonna believe it when we come back with this big chicken-killin' coon; one that big could be a fifteen-dollar coon. Heck, we'll have a bunch of Christmas money when we catch this big 'un. We're gonna catch the biggest coon ever caught in these parts! Let's go get 'em!"

We were deep into the swamp now; our feet and knees were wet, we were scratched up from the blackberry vines, and we were freezing from walking through the snow with thin shoes on and crawling around in the blackberry patch. Sniffer and the coon were long gone—way the heck ahead of us, and we were tired of running after them. We stopped and slapped our hands together trying to warm them up.

"Dang, Richard, I'm tired, cold, and scratched up. Are you sure you wanta keep after that coon? Heck, they must be a half mile ahead, and I can barely hear Sniffer. My jacket's too thin, and my shoes are wet. I've never been this cold and wet in my entire life. I'm ready to quit and go home."

I was thinking the very same thing, when—

"Shussss, listen."

Hoooooooooo! Hoooooooooo! Hoooooooo! Hoo! Hoo! Hoo! Hoo! Hoo!

Sniffer had stopped running! He'd treed the big chicken-killing coon!

"Eeeeeee! Yaaaaaa! Come on! Sniffer's got 'em treed!" We forgot all about being cold, and we took off running as fast as we could in the direction of Sniffer's howling.

As we got closer to Sniffer, we could see Sniffer circling around a big brush top right on the edge of Flat Creek. There was a tall bushy cedar tree right in the middle of the brush top, and we could see something crouched down in the bushy top of the tree.

"I think I see 'em! Look! Up in the top of that little bushy cedar tree! The coon is movin' in the top!" I yelled.

Sure enough, we could see the dark shape of a big coon crawling around between the cedar branches, and every little bit it would growl and snarl.

"Dang, John Clayton; we gotta cross Flat Creek. That tree is on the other side of the creek."

"Heck, Richard, I think the creek's frozen over; let me check it out."

John Clayton eased out on the ice, stood there a few seconds, and then walked on across the creek. "Come on Richard; I weigh fifteen pounds more'n you do. If it'll hold me up, it'll sure hold you."

I eased across the frozen creek, and soon we were struggling through the brush top heading for the bushy cedar tree.

"Come on, John Clayton, let's shake that coon out. Sniffer'll grab it soon as it hits the ground, and if he needs any help we've got these clubs."

"Yeah, but, Richard, that's one big coon. I can't make it out, but it's takin' up most of the top of the tree."

"Yeah, you bet it's a big 'un! It's a world-record coon! Come on, let's get up close to the cedar tree."

The treetop was all that was left of a huge pin oak tree that loggers had cut down last summer. They had carried off the big pin oak logs and left the top of the tree, which had fallen across the cedar tree. There were so many branches around the base of the cedar tree we barely had room to stand up on one side, and the other side was so close to the bank of Flat Creek we couldn't stand there without getting in the water. Finally, me, John Clayton, and Sniffer got ready at the base of the cedar tree where we looked up trying to see the chicken-killing coon which was in the very top of the bushy little tree. Sniffer was so excited he was biting the tree and howling his head off.

"Eeeeeeeeee! Eeeyhaaaaaaa! Git 'em, Sniffer! Sic 'em! Sic 'em!" Sniffer roared and jumped up trying to climb the tree. Old Sniffer went absolutely dog crazy.

"Sniffer's ready, John Clayton, shake the tree! Come outta that tree, Mr. Coon! Eyeeeeeeee! Ahaaaaaa!"

After a few minutes of shaking, we stepped back to think things over. "Shoot, that dang coon's not movin' a bit. The tree's too big to shake. Hey, I've got an idea. Pull out your slingshot and send a few rocks into that bushy part of the tree. I'll bet after a couple of rocks, it'll come outta there."

We pulled out our slingshots and started sending rock after rock into the mass of green cedar branches. Then I heard one of my rocks make a solid thump, and I knew I'd hit the coon. It was moving and then it made a funny sounding snarl.

"Wow! Dang! Did you hear that? That sure sounded like one huge coon!"

"Uh, Richard, that didn't sound like no coon I've ever heard."

"Oh, John Clayton come on; a coon's a coon. It don't matter none how big it is. It's still a dang coon. Get your club ready. Between me, you, and Sniffer we'll take care of that dang coon."

"Come on outta that tree, Christmas money!" John Clayton yelled.

"It's movin'! It's movin'!" I hollered. "Here it comes! Get ready! And don't hit Sniffer!"

I could see the coon crawling through the branches heading down the tree, and we stood there with our clubs raised ready to whap it, while Sniffer just went plumb dog crazy trying to climb that tree.

"Eeeeeeeeeee! Eeeeyhaaaaaaaaaa! Git 'em, Sniffer! Sic 'em! Sic 'em!" Sniffer jumped straight up trying to get to that coon, and then I looked up and—"No! Nooooo! Nooooooooo! It ain't a coon! It ain't a coon! Get outta the way! Oh, my God! Oh, my God! It's not a coon! It's a wildcat! Look out! Here it comes!"

I was trying to back away from the tree when the big eighty-pound wildcat sailed out right at me. Heck, I was trying to get out of the way, but the brush and limbs were so thick, and with me, Sniffer, and John Clayton all huddled around the open space at the bottom of the tree, the wildcat didn't have no place to go, but right in the middle of everybody. You'll never know how scared I was.

Sniffer met the wildcat head on, but after it tore into Sniffer, the hound backed away, and suddenly the cat turned and, before I could move, was all over me. It snarled as it hit me, and I felt a slashing paw rip the sleeve of my coat and shirt as it knocked me backwards, and I sprawled out on the ground. Sniffer, who had backed off after getting chewed up, made a running leap into the pile of boys and wildcat, clomping down on the wildcat.

"Ahaaaaaa! Ahaaaaaa! Run! Run! Run for your life!" I rolled on the ground trying to get out of claw range, and Sniffer tied into a really mad wildcat.

You've never heard such a racket in all your heaven born days; the wildcat snarling, Sniffer howling, and me and John Clayton screaming. The wildcat took another swipe at me, ripping my pants leg and leaving claw marks down my leg before it turned to Sniffer, who had grabbed it by one of its back legs. Sniffer, who knew only one way to finish off a coon, went straight for the wild-cat, knocking it over and jumping right on top of it. Course both me and John Clayton were less than three feet away from that fight, trying to hit the wildcat with our clubs while we tried to stay out of claw range. Sniffer used a pretty good strategy for a big dog trying to finish off a little coon—but not to whip a wildcat. That wildcat flipped over on its back, and four slashing claws and a mouth full of the biggest teeth you've ever seen in your whole entire life hit Sniffer head-on with a snarl like nothing I've ever heard, and old Sniffer looked like he was getting slashed to pieces.

But Sniffer was so fired up he was going after that wildcat like there was no tomorrow, trying to get a grip on its throat. But the dang big wildcat was too much for Sniffer. With a lunge it sent Sniffer rolling back, knocking the legs out from under John Clayton, and the wildcat jumped right on top of Sniffer and John Clayton. Dang, I thought John Clayton was a goner.

"Ahaaaaa! No! No! Get away! Get away!" screamed John Clayton as the rolling and jumping fight was all over him, pinning him against the hedge of broken branches where the swirling fight was all around him.

"Ahaaaa! Oh! Oh! Help, Richard!" Claws and teeth raked his leg, as he fell back into the fallen treetop with Sniffer and the wildcat almost on top of him.

There weren't nothing for me to do but join the fight, which I tried to do by grabbing the leg of the wildcat as it pounced on Sniffer and John Clayton. Boy, was that a stupid thing to do? You dang well know it was. As soon as I grabbed the wildcat's leg it turned and lunged at me, knocking me straight back into the little cedar tree, and when I bounced off the tree, it clawed and bit me. I felt the claws dig into my coat, ripping down the sleeve before Sniffer, thank God, grabbed the wildcat again, and I managed to roll away, tumbling backward onto the ice of frozen Flat Creek, where I hit and slid out to about the middle of the creek. I breathed a sigh of relief, just to be away from the fight, but before I could even move, I heard something cracking.

It was the sound of breaking ice, and before I could get up the ice parted and I sank right to the bottom of the frozen creek. I bobbed up floundering in the coldest water I've ever felt, and I thrashed through the ice to the bank, where I pulled myself out of the water, screaming; "Run! Run! John Clayton! Sniffer can't whip that wildcat! It's gonna kill us all!" I scrambled on all fours up the icy bank calling Sniffer.

"Sniffer! Sniffer! Here! Here!" I was trying to get Sniffer to quit the fight and retreat. Sniffer was more than ready to leave that fight which wasn't going his way at all, but he didn't get very far when the wildcat pounced on him, grabbing him in the middle of his back, and knocking both Sniffer and John Clayton into Flat Creek.

The icy water was boiling now with the dog and wildcat trying to kill each other while John Clayton flopped around right beside them. It was dangdest howling, snarling, and thrashing you've ever seen. John Clayton was screaming bloody murder for help.

"Help! Help! Richard! Help me!" John Clayton screamed as his head popped up out of the water, and he started swimming for the bank as hard as he could.

I jumped in the edge of the water, grabbed John Clayton's hand, pulled him out of the water, and we started to run. I looked over my shoulder and saw that the wildcat had Sniffer in the shallow water about to finish him off.

"Wait, John Clayton; it's gonna kill Sniffer!" If I didn't do something old Sniffer would be one dead dog in a couple of minutes.

I picked up the club I'd brought to help Sniffer whip the coon and ran back to the fight screaming at the top of my lungs.

"Heeee, yaaaaa! Git! Git! Git outta here!" I splashed into the water swinging the club at the big wildcat. I swung as hard as I could and I hit the wildcat across the back twice before it turned Sniffer loose. Finally, with a snarl at me, it dropped Sniffer and ran into the woods.

"Run! Run!" I scrambled out of the creek and started running through the pin oak flat as fast I could run. Sniffer and John Clayton followed, and soon we were a far enough way to stop and catch our breath.

I looked at John Clayton, who looked like a frozen, wet rat, bleeding from the scratches and poor old Sniffer; he'd been chewed on until his ears were just shredded, and my God, he had a claw mark all the way down his nose.

"Oh!—Oh, my God!—Oh, oh, my God!" John Clayton kept muttering over and over again. "Richard! You idiot!—coon!

coon!—You said coon!—Can't you tell the difference between a wildcat and a coon?

"Yeah, I can now, but don't blame me, Mr. Smarty. I saved your sorry hide when I pulled that wildcat off of you."

"No, you didn't, it was Sniffer that saved me, and good gosh; where's Sniffer?"

I looked through the woods and I could barely see Sniffer who had kept running. He didn't want any more of that wildcat fight.

"Oh—I'm so cold—wet—cold." John Clayton muttered again and again.

"Sniffer! Sniffer! Here! Here, boy!" Sniffer reluctantly trotted back still looking at the brush top and letting out one of those hound howls ever few seconds

"Dang, John Clayton, look at Sniffer. He looks like he's been run through a slashin' machine."

Sniffer was whining and shaking his head. His left ear was in shreds, and he had a claw mark that ran from one eye all the way to the end of his nose. His underside was clawed up something terrible, and there was blood running down his back where the wildcat had clamped down on him at the end of the fight, but outside of hurting like heck, all those claw marks weren't gonna kill him.

John Clayton had four claw marks running down his left calf all the way to his ankle, and I had claw marks on my arm and leg. The left arm of my good school coat was in shreds.

We started for my house with a wet, whiny, whimpering dog trailing along behind us, while we sniffed and tried not to cry. We were soaking wet, and the water that soaked our blue jeans was turning into ice. Our feet were so cold they were almost numb, and our fingers were freezing. During the fight, we'd taken off our gloves to shoot our slingshots, and we'd left them under the tree. Now our hands were numb, but even so, we weren't about to go back for those gloves.

"Hurry! John Clayton! We're gonna freeze to death, if we don't get outta these wet clothes!" My fingers had started to get numb.

As we got close to my house I looked over at a frozen-looking John Clayton, who was struggling along in icy covered blue jeans, "Uh, let's give up on tryin' to catch coons to make Christmas money," I said as we struggled through the snow into my back yard.

"Give up? Give up? You stupid idiot! You get us out in the snow and we almost freeze to death; then we get in a fight with a wildcat and nearly get killed, and you say, 'Let's quit tryin' to catch coons.' Just forget Christmas money. We ain't gonna have any."

"Yeah, you're right."

It was about dinnertime, and I was hollering for Momma before I even got to the door.

"Richard! What's wrong?" Momma yelled as she ran out the door. She took one look at a bleeding hound and two cold, wet, scratched-up boys and just shook her head.

"What on God's earth have y'all been into now?"

"Oh, Momma, Sniffer treed the coon, but it weren't no coon. It was a big wildcat, and we got in the middle of the fight with Sniffer and the wildcat and got knocked into Flat Creek. And look at my leg and arm, and poor Sniffer almost got killed."

"Well, let me get your Daddy up. He'll take care of Sniffer while I doctor you and John Clayton." Momma walked back in the house just as Daddy walked out of the bedroom.

"Jack, you won't believe what these boys have been into now." She told him the details while she doctored us. Daddy smiled and finally laughed out loud.

"Y'all looked up in that tree and instead of a coon it was a big wildcat? And y'all all got in a fight with it, and ended up in Flat Creek? Is that right?"

"Yes, sir, but we were in a treetop and we couldn't get outta the way. It knocked us into Flat Creek, and it would've killed Sniffer and John Clayton if I hadn't saved 'em."

"Oh, no, Mr. Mason, Richard was just tryin' to get outta there, and he didn't save nobody but maybe Sniffer. He's just braggin'."

"Yes, I did, I sure did. How do you think I got these claw marks?"

Daddy kept going on how he would have liked to have seen two boys, a skinny hound dog, and a wildcat all fighting like crazy in Flat Creek. He laughed and laughed.

"Jack, I can't believe you're laughing at Richard and John Clayton. They could have been killed or died from frostbite."

"Yeah, Daddy; you should have seen the teeth on that big wildcat. Shoot, he was just about to eat Sniffer and John Clayton when I dove in that frozen creek and grabbed it."

"Liar, liar, liar," mumbled John Clayton.

Momma finally finished with the doctoring, and after standing in front of the fireplace to thaw out, we went into the kitchen for dinner. Boy, was I starving to death, and I couldn't wait to sit down and eat some of Momma's hot cornbread crumbled up in a glass of buttermilk. It's the best cornbread you've ever seen.

After dinner we compared scratches, and except for the big one on Sniffer's nose and the two long ones down my leg, they weren't no big deal, but my good jacket was ripped and torn. Momma shook her head and said she'd try to mend it.

14

Roughnecks and the Newsstand

Sunday, December 17th, 1944

The big snow melted the next day, and I was back delivering those dang sorry papers and going to school. The day after the big snow something really strange happened at the newsstand.

Doc was in his usual bad mood, a-wheeling around yelling at me with his teeth clenched on that cigarette holder, and after a lame excuse cause I was fifteen minutes late, I started running the route. Boy, was I glad when I threw that last paper. I finished the route in almost world-record time that morning, and I was just about to leave the newsstand when the whole crew of roughnecks from Mr. Crotty's drilling rig walked in.

There was something funny about the way they were acting. They spread out; Big Six went behind the candy counter, one went back to the magazine racks, and the other one walked over and started talking to Doc. He got right up in front of Doc and started asking him a bunch of stuff about directions to this and that, and if he carried aspirin and so on. Doc ain't no fool, and he started rolling that wheelchair out in the middle of the room where he could see all of them, but before he could get around the man who was talking to him, Big Six reached in the candy case, grabbed a handful of candy bars, and stuck them in his pocket. I was behind him and saw the whole thing. *Oh, my gosh,* I thought. *Should I say something?* Well, I'll admit Big Six looked so mean, I couldn't get up the nerve to say anything.

Shoot, old Doc was dang sure they were trying to steal stuff, and he was patrolling the newsstand like some Indian scout, but he didn't see Big Six put the candy bars in his pocket. After a few minutes the roughnecks done figured out Doc was a-watching them so close that they couldn't steal nothing else so they started to leave.

Dang, I couldn't stand it no longer and I hollered out, "Doc, Big Six put a handful of candy bars in his pocket while you were talkin' to that other man!" and I pointed to Big Six as he was trying to leave. "He put 'um right there in his front pocket!" Boy, I mean to tell you, I was scared to death when Big Six wheeled around and yelled at me.

"What? You little punk! I didn't take a thang! I just picked up a candy bar and put it right back down, you little liar!"

I was almost frozen in my tracks, but I said, "No, you didn't! You put a whole handful in your pocket! I saw you!" Big Six took a couple of steps toward me and I nearly fainted.

But then Doc got into the action. He bit down on his cigarette holder, and it stood up like a red flag. Then he wheeled his chair around, blocked the door, and grabbed up one of his crutches and got ready to swing.

"Big Six, take those candy bars outta your pocket, and don't any of you come back in this newsstand again!" said Doc as his teeth clenched the cigarette holder until it shook, and if looks could kill, Big Six would have been dead as a sack of hammers.

"Old man, get outta the way or I'm gonna dump you outta that wheelchair right in the floor!" said Big Six. Big Six started toward Doc like he was gonna kill him, and I got really upset.

Oh, my God! I thought. *He's gonna hurt Doc—I gotta do somethin'.*

Doc looked a little nervous, but he drew his crutch back and was about to take a swing at Big Six when I bolted for the back door, yelling, "I'm gonna go get Wing!" Shoot, when I hollered out Wing's name them roughnecks just stopped dead in their tracks.

"Hey, wait a minute, kid!" yelled Big Six. "There ain't no need to go get the law. We's just havin' a little fun." He pulled the candy bars out of his pocket and handed them to Doc. I'd stopped in the back of the newsstand when Big Six yelled out, and I slowly walked back to where Doc was. Everybody just stood there for what seemed like forever, and Big Six stared at me until I almost stopped breathing.

Then Doc rolled his wheelchair back from in front of the door and yelled, "Get outta here, and don't ever step in this newsstand again!"

They backed out the door and the last out, who was Big Six, yelled back at Doc and me, "We're gonna get you both; you better watch out. I don't take kindly to no one a-crossin' me."

Doc looked at me and said, "Worthless trash! Humph, thanks, Richard for calling his hand."

"That's okay, Doc, but they sure looked mean. Ain't you 'fraid they're gonna come back and give us trouble?"

"Naw, that kind is more talk than anything. Wing'll take care of 'em if they set foot in this newsstand again."

"Well, okay, Doc, I hope you're right. See you tomorrow."

I was walking back toward my house when I heard a car coming up behind me. For some reason I looked back and dang; I nearly died of fright. There was an old pickup truck just barreling down the shoulder of the road coming straight at me. "Aaaaah!" I screamed and jumped off the road into the ditch as the truck roared by. "Oh, my good Lord in Heaven!"

It was Big Six and his crew.

The next day I didn't want to go deliver papers, but shoot, what choice did I have? Well, I was late as usual, and I walked in just before the fifteen-minute "no excuse" time. Sniffer plopped down in front of the door to wait on me, and I started to go get the papers when I looked over at Doc who was wheeling around in his wheelchair, and he looked so mad I thought he was gonna explode.

"Doc, what's wrong?"

"Richard, the newsstand has been robbed! Somebody kicked the back door open and smashed my cash register on the floor! Look at the mess!"

It dang sure was a mess all right, and Doc was nearly about hysterical, cause, I mean, Doc can't stand to lose money, and I knew Doc kept about twenty-five dollars in start-up money in his cash register. They had done cleaned him out.

I walked toward the back of the newsstand to the candy counter and the back glass had been busted.

"Look, Doc, they done broke open the candy counter, and a whole box of Baby Ruth candy bars is gone."

"Oh, my God! Dang them!" Doc was spinning his wheelchair around like a top. His cigarette holder was sticking straight up and it was just a-shaking. I ain't never seen him so mad. "Richard, run down to city hall and see if Wing has come to work. Tell him what happened and get him down here quick."

Boy, did I take off running. I dashed out the door and around the corner to city hall just as Wing drove up in his old 1932 Ford.

"Wing! Wing! Doc's been robbed. Somebody done kicked in the back door and busted his cash register."

"What? Are you sure, Richard?"

"Yes sir, and they even busted the candy counter window and swiped a whole box of Baby Ruth candy bars. Doc said for you to hurry over. He ain't gonna clean up the mess 'til you get there."

Wing and I walked back to the newsstand, and for about fifteen minutes Doc cursed the robbers while Wing looked the place over and shook his head.

"Shoot, Doc, there ain't no clues or nothin'. They just kicked down the door and busted your cash register. I'll tell you what though; I'll see Peg later today and if anybody comes in flashin' some new money 'round he'll know 'bout it. Shoot, Peg knows everybody in town, and he knows just how much they spend at the pool hall. If somebody in town did it, we'll find out who it is."

Course that didn't satisfy old Doc. He dang sure wanted his twenty-five dollars back and that box of Baby Ruth candy bars, but Wing finally calmed him down, and I picked up my papers and started out the door. Just before I left the newsstand I walked to the back door to see if the robbers had torn up the door. Sure enough the lock was busted all to heck from a kick which must have been real strong cause there was a big black mark where it hit. I reached over and touched the black mark with my finger.

Huh, it's oil, I thought as I rubbed it between my fingers. *Whoever busted that door down kicked it with an oily boot. Must have been some sorry roughneck in from the drillin' rigs.* Course that would only narrow it down to about a thousand men that worked out in the oil fields. Heck, nearly every man in town probably had oil on their shoes from tramping around in the oil fields.

When I finished my paper route Doc had done cleaned up the mess and even fixed his busted cash register, but boy he was still as mad as a hornet.

"Darn it, Richard, Wing is just worthless! He's the worst excuse for a marshal that I've ever seen! He just wrote down what that sorry bunch took and said we'd be lucky if we ever found out who broke in. You'd think he could do more than that."

"Yeah, Doc, didn't he take no fingerprints or nothin'?"

"Nahaaa, but I'm telling you right now. That's the last time somebody's going to kick the back door open. I'm going to get a door bar put on it today."

I couldn't wait to tell John Clayton about the robbery. Heck, Norphlet never has nothing happen like that. Being the town paperboy I knew just about everybody in town, and I sure couldn't come up with nobody that would do such a thing. But then I thought about them roughnecks that lived in the Womack Boarding House. *Hmmm,* I thought as I walked along throwing the papers; *those are the guys that got in the fight with Bubba down at the City Café, threatened me and Doc, and they sure would have oil on their boots.* Course, I guess I was just thinking about them cause they was such a sorry lot.

The next day after school I talked to John Clayton about the roughnecks, and I told him I found oil on the back door of the newsstand, and how they threatened Doc. He agreed. They were the robbers.

"Shoot, Richard, who else could it be? Have you told Wing?"

"Naw, if I told Wing that I thought it was them, and the only clue I had was the oil on the back door, he'd laugh me outta his office. We need to find some other stuff that would prove they did it, but heck; right now we gotta get Uncle Hugh's groceries before it gets dark."

"Yeah, let's head for the grocery store."

"Uh, look, John Clayton. Here comes Rosalie."

"Ha, get ready to be invisible," laughed John Clayton.

However, instead of walking right by us Rosalie stopped and said hello and smiled at me. Gosh, those blue eyes, they just sparkled. I stood there looking at her with my mouth about half opened. I had a little sick smile on my face.

"Hi, what are y'all up to today?"

"Heck, Rosalie, ain't you heard? Doc done got robbed last night, and we were a-tryin' to figure out who did it," said John Clayton.

"Really? That's great. Who do y'all think did it?"

"Well, Richard thinks he knows who did it. He's done figured it out."

"Richard is gonna solve the robbery? He knows who did it?" said Rosalie. She grinned and looked at me as she shook her head.

"Yeah, Rosalie, he's found some real good clues, and if we can come up with one more little thing, we're gonna get Wing to arrest 'um."

Rosalie looked a little more interested after John Clayton said that.

"Uh, well, yeah, Rosalie; I found oil on the back door and if it matches the oil on that sorry roughneck's boots, I'm gonna have him charged with robbery."

"Huh, well, that would really be something, if it was Big Six and you proved he robbed Doc," she said.

"I just need 'nother couple of clues, Rosalie, and then I'm gonna go get Wing."

"Well, I've got to go. Good luck, Richard."

Rosalie walked away and I stood there still thinking about her blue eyes. I still had that little stupid smile on my face like I do every time I'm around her, and John Clayton spotted it.

"Oh, Richard, you're still moonin' over her."

"Naw, I'm not."

"The heck you ain't. Every time you're 'round her you look like a grinnin' possum."

Well, I hafta admit; for once in his life, John Clayton was right.

I was trying to change the subject when I saw a couple of our friends walking toward us.

"Hey, look; it's Joe Rel and Billy Ray." Joe Rel and Billy Ray, two colored boys, are brothers, and their daddy works at the Norphlet Pipe Yard. They're good friends, and we're always going fishing together.

"Joe Rel, Billy Ray, did y'all hear Doc's Newsstand got robbed last night?" I yelled.

"Yeah," Joe Rel said. "Daddy done come in from a pipe delivery out to the Crotty Drillin' rig, and he said that crew wuz talkin' 'bout it. Said they was laughin' 'bout poor old Doc gettin' robbed."

Uh? I thought. *How'd they know?*

"Hey, wait a minute; how in the heck did they know Doc had been robbed? They've been on that rig since six this mornin', and the robbery was last night."

"Shoot, I don't know, Richard, but they show knowed it."

I looked at John Clayton, and he was nodding his head.

After Joe Rel and Billy Ray headed on down to the store, John Clayton piped up: "Heck, Richard, now we know dang well they did it, but shoot, Wing ain't gonna arrest 'um cause we think they did it. We need some more evidence."

"Yeah, you're right."

The next morning I turned down Front Street as I delivered papers, and as I walked in front of the Womack Boarding House, Sniffer ran over to the garbage can sitting on the curb and started nosing through the trash.

"Sniffer, get outta that trash!" I yelled, just as Sniffer pulled out something and started chewing on it.

"Sniffer, put that down!" I walked over, whacked him on the head with a newspaper, and Sniffer dropped what he had been chewing on. I looked down, and there was a half-eaten Baby Ruth candy bar.

"What?" I started looking through the trash, and sure enough it was full of Baby Ruth candy wrappers. I even found the Baby Ruth box that the candy had come in.

"Oh, my gosh, this stuff is from Doc's," I muttered. Heck, I knew right then that there weren't no doubt that them rough-necks staying in the Womack Boarding House had robbed Doc.

I put all the wrappers and the box in my paper bag and headed back for the newsstand. Doc didn't need to know about this until I told Wing. Shoot, he'd get all worked up and carry on like nothing you've ever seen. I figured maybe Wing would arrest them and get Doc's money back, and then Doc could just be glad Wing caught them.

That afternoon me and John Clayton sat around and talked about whether we should give Wing the evidence right then or try to find out some more stuff about the robbers. Heck, we both knew they did it, but we thought we might need a little more evidence.

Finally, I said to John Clayton, "Let's go over and talk to Peg and see if he has noticed if those roughnecks have been spendin' more money with him."

"Yeah," said John Clayton, "Peg's a good friend, and he'll tell us everythin'." We walked down to Peg's Place and yelled in the door for Peg.

In a couple of minutes Peg came out. He was carrying his coffee can to spit tobacco in, and his wild gray hair was sticking out from under an old beat-up felt hat. He had an old blue workshirt on under his overalls. That's Peg's winter outfit. In the summer Peg just wears his overalls and nothing else.

"Boys, what can I do for y'all?" Peg said as he spit tobacco juice in the coffee can.

"Peg, you know Doc got robbed the other night?"

"Yeah, I told the tight old fart he shoulda had a bar on that back door years ago. He'll squeeze a nickel so tight he suffocates the buffalo."

I said, "Uh, well, Peg, we think we know who did the robbery."

"Naw, you don't."

"Uh, huh."

"Really? Who?"

Then I told Peg about the roughnecks threatening Doc, finding oil on Doc's back door, Joe Rel's daddy telling that the roughnecks knew about the robbery, and then finding the Baby Ruth candy bar wrappers in the garbage outside the Womack Boarding House, "Peg," I said, "have them three sorry roughnecks that got in the fight with Bubba been in here spendin' extra money?"

"Huh? Well, Richard, now that you mention it, they shore has. In fact I nearly dropped my teeth yesterday when that worthless bunch of fools bought beer for a whole table of domino players. Maybe y'all got something here. Hey, by the way, if you see Bubba tell him they're still mighty mad 'bout that fight with the skillet. I overheard one of them say they was gonna catch 'em when he got off from work some night and beat the fool outta him with a two by four, and it sounded like the way they talked it was gonna be real soon. Maybe you need to go down to Wing's office and tell him what y'alls come up with, and tell him about Bubba. I gotta get back inside, some loud-mouth son-of-a-gun is hollerin' for 'nother beer."

Peg walked back in the pool hall, and me and John Clayton looked at each other.

"There ain't no doubt them roughnecks broke into Doc's, and now they're gonna beat up Bubba," I said. "Let's go tell Wing."

We ran around the corner to the town marshal's office, where we found Wing leaning back in his chair asleep.

"Wing! Wing!" I yelled. "We know who broke into Doc's."

"What? Huh."

Wing woke with a start, sat up, smiled, and said, "Now boys, y'all got some pretty big imaginations, but what have y'all come up with to make you think you know who broke into Doc's?"

For the next few minutes we stood there waving our arms, telling Wing about all the evidence we'd come up with. At first

Wing just smiled, but then as I got to the candy bar wrappers and the box they came in, Joe Rel's Daddy hearing about the robbery out on the rig, and finally when I told him about what Peg had said he pulled his chair forward, nodding his head.

"Dang, boys, y'all might be on to something, and you said Peg overheard 'um say they was gonna beat up on old Bubba after work?"

"Yes, sir, Peg said from the way they talked it might be real soon."

"We'll see about that," Wing said as he got up. "Come on boys, y'all can walk over to the boardin' house and watch me arrest that bunch of trash."

Wow, Wing started for the door twirling his blackjack, and I looked at John Clayton. We couldn't wait 'til Wing made the arrest. Heck, we was just a-hoping Wing would get to use his blackjack, especially on that sorry Big Six who tried to run me down.

15

Marshal Wing Makes the Arrest

Tuesday, December 19th, 1944

While we were walking over to the boarding house I thought of something. "Wing, after you arrest those guys, will you tell Doc I solved the robbery?"

"You bet, Richard, but don't look for no reward from Doc. Heck, if you get a Baby Ruth or a funny book, you'll be doin' good. You know Doc's as tight as a tick on a hound's back end."

I smiled and nodded at John Clayton.

"What?" he said.

"Just wait," I whispered. "I done got a plan."

Pretty soon we came to the Womack Boarding House, where Mrs. Womack was a-sitting out on the porch reading a newspaper. She was plopped down in an old metal yard chair, which looked like it was ready to collapse, cause, you know, she's a large woman. Heck, she ain't just large; she's big as the side of a barn.

"How are you, Mrs. Womack?" Wing said. "I come by to talk with a couple of your boarders. Is them roughneck that works on the Crotty rig in?"

"I'm fine, Wing, but they ain't here. They's workin' daylights, and ain't gonna be back 'til dark. Whatcha wanta talk with them 'bout?"

"Oh, just 'bout some stuff. Nothin' big. What time do they usually get in?"

"Depends, Wing; sometime they comes in right from work 'round six o'clock, but I don't think they's gonna be in real quick tonight. They told me this mornin' they wouldn't make supper. I'd look for 'um 'round nine. Said they had somethin' to take care of after work."

Wing nodded, and I looked at John Clayton. We all knew them sorry roughnecks were gonna wait on Bubba and beat the fool out of him when he got off work.

"All right, I'll come back later. Thank you, Mrs. Womack."

"Don't mention it, Wing."

Wing looked at us as we walked away. "Boys, don't y'all worry none 'bout Bubba, I'll be waitin' in the alley when he gets off, and if that bunch of roughnecks goes after him, I'll work 'um over with this blackjack. Now y'all go on home. I'll tell you 'bout it tomorrow."

"Yes, sir." We walked back toward the newsstand, but we were thinking about how much we'd like to watch Wing arrest that sorry bunch.

John Clayton must have been thinking the same thing. "Say, Richard, I'd give anything in the whole wide world just to see Wing arrest those guys. I'll bet he'll use his blackjack. Wow, would that be somethin' to watch."

"You bet it would. Say, I've got an idea; let's meet down here after supper. I'll tell Momma I'm gonna go over to your house to get some homework, and you can do the same. We'll meet at the breadbox, sneak over, and watch the alley. Bubba gets off work at eight, and as soon as he hangs up his apron, he'll come out the back door of the café."

"Hey, that sounds great. I'll meet you at the breadbox about seven-thirty."

Ever since Wing had started trying to arrest those guys, I'd been thinking about something. "Okay, but first I need to do somethin'. Come on, let's go in the newsstand. I gotta talk with Doc 'fore I go home."

"You ain't gonna tell him 'bout Wing fixin' to arrest those guys are you?"

"Heck, no, but you just listen to what I'm gonna tell Doc, and help me out." I gave John Clayton a big grin.

"Huh?"

We walked in and Doc, who'd been in a real sorry mood ever since the robbery, wheeled his chair around and glared at us.

Man, that cigarette holder popped straight up, and you could hear him snort.

"Humph."

"Doc, have they caught the crooks that robbed you?" I asked.

"Well, no, that dang worthless Wing's not doin' a thing but sleepin' in that office chair."

"Heck, Doc, maybe you outta offer up a reward to anybody that gets 'um arrested."

"Oh, my gosh!" whispered John Clayton. He put his hand over his mouth to keep from laughing out loud. "Yeah, Doc, maybe a hundred dollars," he piped up.

"A hundred dollars? Are you crazy? They only took twenty-five dollars and a box of Baby Ruths."

"Well, heck, Doc," I said, "I'm always seein' posters and hearin' stuff on the radio about people offerin' up a reward, but I guess they wanta catch their crooks a lot more'n you want to catch the guys that busted in here."

"Oh no they don't! By God, I wanta see those thieves rot in jail, and if somebody gets 'um caught, shoot, I'd sure reward 'um."

"How much, Doc?" I said, trying to hold back a smile.

"Richard, I'd give ten dollars to anybody that gets 'um caught."

"Oh, Doc, ain't near 'nough, heck, you need to come up with more'n that," said John Clayton.

"Humph, well maybe, just maybe, I'd throw in another five dollars, if those rascals were thrown in jail."

I smiled and nodded my head. "Well, we gotta go, Doc, I'll see you in the mornin'."

"Richard, for once in your life; try to be on time."

"Sure, Doc, I will."

"Humph."

We walked out of Doc's with John Clayton about to bust. When we were out of earshot he cackled; "Oh, my gosh, I can't wait 'til tomorrow. If Wing arrests those guys, and tells Doc you found the evidence, old Doc is gonna have a danged heart attack if he hasta give you fifteen dollars."

"Yeah, and I'm gonna be on time for the paper route. That'll really shock 'em."

After supper I walked into the kitchen where Momma and Daddy were listening to Walter Winchell and said; "Momma, I need to go over and see John Clayton. He's got some *World Books* that I need to look up somethin' for school." Well, Walter Winchell had just started talking about the war, and I could've asked for the moon and Momma would have just nodded.

As I left the room I could hear Walter Winchell's voice filling the kitchen.

"Good evening Mr. and Mrs. North and South America and all the ships at sea—let's go to press—Germans are on their last leg, war to be over soon—"

I could still hear him as I walked across the yard and headed for town.

John Clayton walked up to the breadbox about half past seven, and we slipped across the street to the back of the old Central Hotel, where we stood in the alley, out of sight, inside a dark doorway and waited for Bubba to get off work. There was a streetlight near the sidewalk and its dim light cast a glow down the alley. Almost at the other end of the alley was the back entrance to the Red Star Drug Store, and the light over the door lit up the back part of the alley.

I'm not a-scared of the dark, but that creepy alley and the cobwebs hanging down inside that doorway made the hair stand up on the back of my neck. I backed up against the door, and a roach got in my hair. Dang, I nearly came unglued slapping at my hair. About ten minutes later Big Six and the other two roughnecks turned off the street and started walking down the alley, carrying two by four pieces of lumber. We got way back in the dark doorway as they passed.

Big Six pointed to one side of the café door and the other two roughnecks walked over and crouched beside it.

Big Six whispered across to the other two men, "Y'all wait 'til I hit 'em, then jump in, and we'll teach that big idiot a lesson or two." Big Six moved across and stood against the wall on the other side of the door. I glanced back down the alley and saw Wing peek around the corner and then step back out of the alley.

It weren't but a few minutes 'til I heard the back door of the café open, and I looked across the alley to see Bubba step out and start to light a cigarette.

"Git 'em!" yelled Big Six. He swung his two by four at Bubba, who never saw it coming.

Oh, my God! I thought.

"Ahaaaaa!" screamed Bubba.

Bubba didn't see the first lick from Big Six's two by four that hit him across the back and knocked him to his knees. But shoot, Bubba wasn't out of the fight yet. He swung and hit Big Six right below his belt and tackled the one of them other roughnecks, and in a few seconds there was the durnest fight you ever did see as Bubba tried to whip three guys armed with two by fours. He was doing some good too, beating one of the guys' head against the ground, but the other two kept beating him with the two by fours, and I could see real quick that Bubba had met his match, and if somebody didn't stop the fight, Bubba was gonna get beat half to death. Them roughnecks was just about to finish him off when Wing stepped into the light and pointed to the three men.

"Stop that fightin'! Stop it! Do you hear me?" he shouted as he ran up the alley to where the fight was taking place.

"You three! You're under arrest!" Wing said to roughnecks. He was twirling his blackjack as he walked up to the three men.

The fighting stopped, and Bubba crawled to his knees as the three guys, shocked at being caught, stared at Wing. Wing has a big .45-caliber pistol, but it was still in its holster. I guess a one-armed man with just a blackjack didn't look that tough to those guys. They looked at each other, and Big Six said, "We ain't going nowheres with you, fellow. Now just get your butt outta this alley, and we'll go back to takin' care of our business."

As Big Six said that, he made a wild swing with his two by four at Wing, who stepped aside, and then—wow, I heard Big

Six's head crack when Wing's blackjack flashed out. Wing's first lick caught Big Six on the side of his head, and before he could even fall, two more licks knocked him across the alley. He dropped like a rock, and the two by four he was beating Bubba with rattled over and landed right in front of the doorway where we were standing.

Shoot, I thought it was gonna be all over in a minute cause Wing waded into the other two with his blackjack a-swinging. One of them men held his hand up and caught the blackjack right on his wrist. Man, that blackjack busted his wrist so quick it'd make your head swim.

"Ahaaaaa! Oh, ahaaaa!"

It was going real good for Wing cause that lick had just about put another man out of the fight, but as Wing was about to finish him off, the other man, who still had his two by four, swung and caught Wing across his shoulder and Wing staggered back against the brick wall clutching his shoulder. I could tell Wing was hurt real bad, and he looked kinda out of it.

"By God, you sorry son-of-a-gun, you're gonna regret jumpin' into this fight!" yelled the man as he started for Wing with the two by four pulled back.

About that time I heard Bubba yell and he grabbed the man that had the busted wrist and slammed him into the brick wall not two feet from Wing.

"Ahaaaaa! Oh, stop, stop!" the roughneck screamed as he fell on the ground, still holding his wrist.

The man that was about to hit Wing with the two by four stopped for just a second as he watched Bubba go over and start stomping the man he'd thrown into the wall. In a couple of seconds the roughneck with the two by four turned away from Bubba and drew back to nail Wing, who was almost helpless, leaning back against the brick wall.

"Oh, my God, John Clayton, Wing's in trouble," I whispered. "What are we gonna do?" Then I looked down and spotted the two by four Big Six had dropped when Wing hit him with the blackjack. I snatched it up and with one swing I hit the man that was about to kill Wing, right in the middle of his back.

"Ahaaaaa! Dang you!" he screamed as he turned to see who had hit him.

That was all the time Wing needed as he took a step forward.

Wing's blackjack whipped through the air, catching the stunned man right above his jaw, and Wing didn't stop until the man slumped to the ground with blood streaming out of his mouth. Finally Wing gave him a kick and looked over at Bubba.

"Bubba, quit stompin' that man. Let me put these handcuffs on 'em."

Bubba gave the man, who was just about stone cold, a last kick as Wing reached down and handcuffed him. I looked around; Big Six was still knocked out cold as a cucumber as was the last man Wing had hit, and the man with the busted wrist was barely wiggling.

Wing finished up the handcuffing and turned around and looked over at me and John Clayton. "Boys, what in the world are y'all doing here? You know I told y'all I'd take care of this bunch." Then Wing smiled and gave me a little hug. "Well, thanks for the help, Richard. Dang, you hit that sorry son-of-a-gun pretty hard. Now you boys go on home. I'll call the sheriff and get this sorry lot locked up. Heck, even if they didn't rob Doc, they assaulted me and Bubba. That'll get 'um sent up to Tucker pen for a few years."

"Yeah, Wing, but you know they really did rob Doc. See if they still have any of Doc's money in their pockets."

"Well, I gotta search 'um anyways. Let's see what they have in their pockets."

Wing pulled out a couple of old beat-up billfolds and looked inside. It was Big Six's billfold that Wing looked in first.

"Hmmm, fifteen dollars, and dang, look what else is in the sorry rascal's pocket, a half-eaten Baby Ruth. Heck, ain't no doubt 'bout it. they're guilty as sin."

He opened the next billfold and pulled out another ten dollars and stuffed the money in his pocket.

"I'll stop by Doc's and give 'em his money back in the morning."

"Wing, be sure to tell Doc that I got 'em arrested," I said as Wing started back to his office to call the sheriff.

"Heck, I sure will, Richard. Doc's gonna be real excited to find out you helped get his money back."

John Clayton couldn't help from smiling as he said, "Yeah, Doc's gonna be excited all right. I just wish I could be there."

Me and John Clayton split up and headed for home. I lay in the bed that night with a big smile on my face. I couldn't wait for that alarm to ring. *Christmas money!—Gollee, Big Six is gonna get me that red scarf.* That was my last thought before I drifted off.

It seemed I'd just gone to sleep when that danged alarm clock went off. I hit the floor pulling on my pants, and in a few minutes me and Sniffer were running for the newsstand. Boy, talk about excited; I couldn't wait to deliver them papers and get back to the newsstand.

"Look at the clock, Doc!" I yelled as I walked through the door. "I'm on time!"

Doc looked up, surprised, and glanced at the big clock over his desk.

"Well, not exactly, Richard, but three minutes late is exceptional for you."

Wow, was I in a good mood. I finished my route by around six-thirty and went in the back behind the candy counter to wait on Wing, who would be by Doc's after he picked up a cup of coffee at the City Café. Doc was still in a terrible mood about the robbery, and he was muttering something about calling the State Police.

I was sitting in the back of the newsstand reading a funny book when I saw Wing walking toward the newsstand. He opened the door and smiled at Doc. "Told you we'd get that sorry bunch that robbed you." He pulled out the twenty-five dollars he'd taken from the roughnecks and slapped it down on Doc desk.

Doc was wide-eyed and so excited he could hardly stand it.

"Yes! Yes! I hope they get sent up!" he hooted and wheeled his chair around. His cigarette holder was bobbing around like a fishing pole.

Wing stuck his thumb in his pants and leaned back against the door.

"They's as good as in Tucker pen right now," Wing crowed.

Wing looked back behind the candy counter where I was still reading a funny book, playing like I hadn't heard all the talk about catching the robbers.

"Richard, come out here!" hollered Wing.

I walked around the candy counter and stood there right beside Wing, trying to keep from smiling. Doc was just reaching out to pick up his money when Wing started talking.

"Doc, you need to thank Richard. This boy came up with the evidence that solved this case."

"Huh?" Doc's hand stopped right above the money.

"Yep, he sure as heck did. He checked the door and found oil on it where someone had kicked it down, and then he found a whole bunch of Baby Ruth wrappers in the trash down at the Womack Boarding House. Shoot, I even found a half of a Baby Ruth in one of those guy's pockets. Doc, Richard's the one that got 'um caught."

When Wing said that, Doc's hand slowly moved back from the money, and as Wing went on and on I could see Doc's face turn from a big smile to a frown as he stared down at his twenty-five dollars. His cigarette holder drooped down.

"Shoot, Doc, you autta give Richard a funny book for solvin' this case."

Doc's face lit up as he thought maybe he'd get off light, but I turned to Wing and said, "Uh, well, Doc has offered up a big reward to anyone who gets them robbers 'rrested."

"Really, Doc?"

Doc was squirming around now and his cigarette holder really began to sag. He really didn't know what to say.

"Did you offer a reward, Doc?" Wing said. He leaned over 'til he was right in Doc's face.

"Uh, maybe," Doc finally said. He plopped back in his chair, and his cigarette holder dropped down against his chin.

"Maybe? What the heck does 'maybe' mean?"

"Well," Doc sighed, "the other morning while Richard and John Clayton were in here talking about catching the robbers I did mention a reward, but—"

"Hold up, Doc." Wing said. "How much did you mention?"

"Uh, ten dollars—"

I held up my hand and shook my head. "No, Doc, remember, you said you'd give another five dollars if those robbers were jailed, and they're in jail right now. Right, Wing?"

"They dang sure are, Doc. Now was it ten dollars or fifteen?"

Doc mumbled something that I couldn't make out and Wing smiled, "That sounded like fifteen to me," and he reached down and picked up a ten and a five and handed them to me.

"Thanks, Doc! Wow, fifteen dollars! I ain't never had that much money at one time in my whole entire life!"

Doc reached out to the table and grabbed up the ten dollars that was still left and stuck it in his cash register.

"Dang, Wing caught the sorry bunch, and you're walking away with more money than I got back," Doc mumbled through gritted teeth as he bit down on his cigarette holder, and then—*Crack!*—Doc had bitten it in half. I tried not to laugh, but Wing just cackled as Doc sat there and fumed.

I thought it'd be a good time to get out of there since Wing was still around, and Doc might decide to call off the reward if he could figure any way around it.

"I gotta go, see you in the mornin', Doc."

I sprinted for the door and headed for school before Doc could answer.

"My Christmas money! My Christmas money!" It kept just flooding through my mind as I ran to school. By the time I got to the school yard, I'd divided out the money in my head and picked out presents for everybody on my list. The red scarf for Rosalie was item number one.

Gosh, solving a real robbery and getting a reward; I couldn't wait to tell everybody. I made it to the school yard about fifteen minutes early and ran up to John Clayton.

"Look at this!" I yelled as I took out the fifteen-dollar reward and waved it around.

"My gosh, I can't believe Doc actually gave you the reward!"

"Yeah, Wing was great, tellin' Doc how I solved the case."

Me and John Clayton had been standing there talking for about ten minutes when Rosalie walked by, and John Clayton ran over to her yelling about me solving the robbery. I was standing there holding the fifteen dollars in my hand when she walked over.

"Richard! I can't believe it! That's wonderful!"

I stood there embarrassed, but really, I was tickled to death. Rosalie kept going on about me solving the robbery, and I just stood there smiling and holding out the fifteen dollars for everyone to see. Then, to my surprise, Rosalie reached out and took my hands while we stood there talking. Wow, John Clayton was even surprised, and I knew right then and there that me and Rosalie were gonna be boyfriend and girlfriend.

Wait 'til Christmas, I thought. *She's really gonna be surprised when I give her that red scarf.*

When Rosalie walked away, all I could think about was that red scarf I was gonna get her for Christmas. Now I had fifteen dollars, and when I put that with my paper route money I'd have over twenty. I spent the last thirty minutes of class making out my Christmas present list.

Finally school was out and I headed home to show Momma and Daddy the reward money, and tell them about solving the newsstand robbery. When I got home Momma was at the sewing machine trying to sew up my jacket that the wildcat had ripped up. She shook her head as I walked in.

"Richard, I can't fix the jacket. It's torn all the way through the lining, and it'll never be right mended. We're just going to have to get you a new jacket, but I don't know where on earth we'll find the money to do it."

At that moment, I could care less about a jacket. In fact it had warmed up a bunch since the big snow, and I hadn't even needed a jacket for the last few days. I figured Momma was gonna be all excited just like Rosalie when I told her about solving the robbery. I couldn't wait to tell her.

"Uh, Momma, guess what?"

"I don't know Richard. What?"

"I solved the newsstand robbery, and Doc gave me a fifteen-dollar reward."

Momma's eyes lit up, and then it hit me. *Oh, no, not my fifteen dollars,* I thought as I tried to back away and leave the room before Momma could say those dreaded words. I didn't make it out of the room in time.

"Richard, that's wonderful. We can get you a new jacket down at Camel's Dry Goods, and with your fifteen-dollar reward money we can almost pay for it."

"No, Momma, no; I don't need no jacket. It's warmed up."

Mamma frowned, and I knew what was coming. Grammar lesson again.

"You don't need what?"

"Uh, well; well, I don't need any jacket."

"A jacket," Momma said.

"Yes ma'am."

"Richard, you know we've still got January and February to go, and you've got to have a jacket. Now, hand me the money." Momma gave me one of them *I ain't foolin'* looks, and I knew it weren't no use to argue.

It was a lost cause. I'd caused my jacket to be ripped up, and now with fifteen dollars in my hand I didn't have a choice except to hand it to Momma.

When I reached out to hand Momma the reward money, all I could think about was the red scarf. I felt a moment of panic cause I dang sure knew it would cost more than the five dollars I had left from my paper route, and when Momma grabbed holt of the money I just couldn't turn loose.

"Richard? Richard? Turn loose of the money."

I finally did, and when the money slipped through my fingers

I just felt sick at my stomach.

So, dang, I had my Christmas money, but in a few seconds it just flat disappeared into Momma's purse. Well, I moped around the house for the rest of the afternoon, but then I thought about how cold I'd be the rest of the winter without a coat, and I figured having a new coat, as cold as it had been this winter, ain't all that bad.

16

The Perfect Christmas Tree

Thursday, December 21st, 1944

Thursday morning Momma walked over to where I was eating breakfast and said, "Richard, I want you and John Clayton to go cut a Christmas tree this afternoon."

"Sure, Momma, I saw a bunch of cedars over on the back fence row. I'll get John Clayton, and we'll go get one this afternoon." I was tickled at the idea of hunting a Christmas tree. There's something about cutting down a cedar tree and dragging it home that makes Christmas seem real.

"That's fine, Richard. I want to start decorating it tonight."

John Clayton came over, we picked up my hatchet, and soon we were traipsing across the big field behind my house heading for a row of cedar trees that were growing along the edge of the fence. Course I was looking for the perfect Christmas tree, but all I could think about was having to use my reward money for a new coat and not having enough money left to buy Rosalie the red scarf. Finally, I got Rosalie off my mind and started thinking about Christmas trees. I knew Momma wanted a perfectly shaped seven- or eight-foot cedar; not no spangley pine.

The walk across the field didn't take but a few minutes and soon we were looking at a row of cedar trees from three to ten feet tall.

"Come on, Richard, pick one out. We ain't got all day."

"I'm lookin'. I'm lookin', but they're bushy on one side and bare on the other. These trees ain't gonna work. Momma always puts the tree right in the middle of the room, and it'll look terrible with a bare side. Let's go over by old man Odom's farm. I 'member seein' some big cedars when we were checkin' out his watermelon patch last summer."

We crossed through a pine thicket and came out on the edge of old man Odom's back field. John Clayton stood there, smiling.

"Hey, Richard, remember last summer runnin' across this field with them hounds after you and hearin' that shotgun blast away?"

"Yeah," I nodded and smiled. "Me and Ears was a-runnin' for our lives carryin' that big watermelon, but shoot, forget 'bout that dang watermelon raid. We're here just to cut a little fence-row cedar. We'll be helpin' 'em out by clearin' his fence-row. Look over there, John Clayton. There's a whole bunch of cedars."

We looked and looked for the perfect tree, but every tree was bare on one side or crooked or something was wrong.

"Dang, Richard, you're so picky. How 'bout this one?"

"Naw, shoot, that back side's almost bare." Finally, we gave up and started up the lane beside old man Odom's yard. Just as we were about to pass his house, I grabbed John Clayton's arm and pointed to a cedar tree.

"Look, John Clayton, that's our Christmas tree!" And it sure was. It was an eight-foot cedar that was perfectly shaped.

"Are you kidding? It's in old man Odom's front yard. That ain't no wild tree and you know it."

"Huh, it's over at the edge of his yard; maybe it came up and as much as old man Odom likes to clear land, he ain't got 'round to cuttin' that tree."

"Richard, you know bettern that."

We stood there and looked at that tree for about five minutes and then walked on back down the road toward my house. I couldn't get that perfect Christmas tree off my mind. *The absolutely perfect tree,* I thought, *just sittin' there waitin' to be cut.* It seemed the more I thought about it, the more I wanted it.

Finally, I looked at John Clayton and said, "It'll be dark in 'bout thirty minutes and we're goin' back and get that tree. Heck, old man Odom don't give a flip 'bout trees. He probably won't even care if we cut that one."

"What? You're crazy. You know dang well he'd care if someone cut a tree right outta his front yard. He'll hear you and that dang shotgun will be rainin' birdshot down on you before you can get ten feet. For God's sake, Richard, after nearly gettin' shot last summer, I'd think you'd know better than to fool with that old man."

I was smiling now, cause I'd thought of a plan.

"Naw, he won't shoot us cause he ain't gonna hear us."

"Whatcha you mean by 'us'? I ain't 'bout to help cut that tree down. Man, one lick with your hatchet, and he'd be out there after us. I may be dumb, but I ain't cold chicken stupid."

"Yeah, maybe, but what if he didn't hear nothin'?"

"Huh?"

"Yeah, I'll use Daddy's saw and cut it real slow where he won't hear a sound. He'll never know a thing 'til tomorrow morning, and we'll done have the perfect Christmas tree."

"I don't know, Richard. It still sounds crazy."

"Come on, you chicken. At least watch the house for me. Let's go get the saw."

John Clayton whined about how mean old man Odom was for a few minutes, but finally he agreed to watch the house while I cut the tree and pulled it out of the yard.

"This is gonna be so easy."

John Clayton shook his head but followed me out to the barn.

We walked back to the barn and got Daddy's saw and started back up the road. It was dark as we approached old man Odom's front yard.

"Shusss," I whispered. "Follow me, and don't make a sound."

Old man Odom had a fenced-in front yard with a big iron gate facing his porch steps. His house had a long porch, and Mrs. Odom had planted a rose garden along the side of the porch. I figured if we could sneak through the gate and crawl on the ground to the porch steps, then we'd be behind the rosebushes until we got to the cedar tree. However, there was one danged problem; the weather had warmed up a bunch over the past week and old man Odom had his front door open. I had second thoughts right then and there: *Go back, Richard. This is a dumb idea.* But, you know, I didn't stop. I just kept crawling along, with John Clayton tugging at my pants leg trying to get me to turn around.

I eased open the front gate and we crawled across the ground 'til we were even with the porch steps.

"Shussss, I can see old man Odom sittin' in the livin' room listenin' to the radio." We crept past his front window and slipped behind the rosebushes.

John Clayton grabbed my arm and whispered, "Richard! Stop! Stop! This is crazy!" But I just kept on crawling 'til I was right beside the tree. John Clayton was breathing little short breaths, and he looked as scared as a head-lighted rabbit, but after I poked him, he turned around and sat watching the front door while I started to saw. As I sawed the tree I could smell the fresh cedar and old man Odom's fireplace. *Boy, it sure smells like Christmas,* I thought. I stopped sawing for a minute and just sat there thinking. *This'll be a great Christmas tree. Dang, if only I could buy Rosalie that scarf, Christmas would be perfect.* Then I started back sawing.

Everything was going pretty good, and I almost had the tree cut when old man Odom got up and walked out on his front porch. When that screen door banged I almost had a heart attack.

Oh, my God. I thought. *He's gonna see us.*

John Clayton punched me, I stopped sawing, and we flattened out on the ground. *This is it,* I thought. *We're goners.*

For a couple of minutes old man Odom walked up and down his porch, stretched, and then put a big chew of tobacco in his mouth. He was less than six feet from us, as we held our breath and prayed he didn't look down. Finally, after hacking and coughing for a few minutes, he spit a mouthful of tobacco juice off the porch and walked back in.

Thank God! I thought as I breathed a sigh of relief.

"Ahaaa, I've got tobacco juice on my leg," John Clayton hissed. "Dang you, Richard, let's get outta here." He grabbed my arm and started to pull me, but I took one look at the tree and shook my head.

"Naw, I've almost finished." I started to saw again, and the tree started to sway. I poked John Clayton. "Hey, get ready. It's about to fall." I gave the tree a little push, and what happened then still gives me nightmares.

The loudest *Pop!* and *Crack!* that you ever did hear echoed through the still night, and John Clayton jumped straight up.

"Oh! Oh! Oh, Richard, he heard that! Let's get outta here!" He scrambled along on his stomach toward the gate.

I looked in the house just as old man Odom tuned his head toward the door and started to get up.

"Run, Richard! He's comin'! He's comin'!" John Clayton hissed frantically as he opened the iron gate, but I was already pulling the tree out of the yard.

"Help me! Grab on to one side of the tree!" I whispered as I pulled the tree along and started toward his gate.

"Drop the tree, Richard! You idiot! He's gonna catch us if you don't! Drop it! For God's sake, drop the tree!" John Clayton was beginning to panic.

"No, I'm takin' the tree. Help me! Grab the tree, John Clayton. We're gonna take this tree home! Now, hurry!"

I heard the screen door slam as old man Odom walked out on his front porch. The eight-foot cedar tree went out the gate as he stood there in shock. My heart was beating ninety miles an hour.

"What? What in the Sam Hill is goin' on? Hey, come back here with that tree!" he yelled and stomped his feet on the wooden porch.

"Dang, you worthless kids, you're gonna be sorry for tryin' to steal my cedar tree! Elsie! Elsie! Hand me my shotgun. It's sittin' by the fireplace!" he yelled as he stuck his head in the doorway.

"Oh, my God! Oh, my God! Run! Run for your life, John Clayton, and help me with this tree!" We made it out of the yard and started for the highway.

Finally, John Clayton grabbed one of the lower limbs, and we were hightailing it down the road as fast as we could run and drag a Christmas tree. I heard old man Odom's screen door slam again and footsteps as he ran across the porch. Then both barrels of old man Odom's shotgun echoed through the night. The first shot went ripping through the bushes along the road and the second shot whistled overhead.

He'd missed, but not by much. I swear to the good Lord above, I've never, ever been as scared in my entire life. *We're goners,* I thought. *Thank God it's dark!* "Faster! Faster, John Clayton!" I yelled. "Run! Run!"

John Clayton was whining up a storm. "Oh, my God! Oh, my God! He's gonna kill us!"

"Shut up and run, we're almost out of range!" I tried to pick up a little more speed before old man Odom could reload. We were pulling that tree right down the middle of the highway, running as fast as we could, when that shotgun boomed out again.

"Oh, my God!" screamed John Clayton, cause even though we was nearly out of range birdshot was raining out of the sky all around us.

"Oh, dang, dang! I'm hit! Aaaaah!" John Clayton screamed. Then topping the hill came a car heading our way, and we looked like a couple of deer in the headlights as we ran.

Evidently old man Odom could see us in the car headlights dragging the tree down the road, because that last round was right on target. Little pieces of shot peppered us from our head to our feet. Most of them bounced off cause we were almost out of range, but a couple hit my bare leg and they stung like heck. We hollered, yelled, and dodged the car as we pulled the Christmas tree down the highway.

We were moaning and whining to beat sixty by the time we got back to my house.

"Richard, if I don't die from this birdshot, I'm gonna kill you for gettin' us into this!"

"Stop whinin', John Clayton, and let's go into my bedroom and see how bad we got hit." We dropped the Christmas tree in my back yard and ran through the house to my bedroom.

"Momma, we got a Christmas tree. It's in the back yard. Me and John Clayton are goin' into my room," I yelled as we ran through the kitchen.

Momma walked out the door to look at the Christmas tree, and we went in my bedroom and closed the door.

We sat on my bed gasping for breath, shaking like leaves. Then I said, "Take off your shirt and let me see your back."

John Clayton pulled his shirt off. He had a few little red spots where the shot had hit, but none of them had broken the skin.

"Richard, I'm bleedin' up on my neck."

"Hmmm, yeah, you are. It looks like one of them shot broke the skin and is buried just under the skin. Hold still."

"Ahaaa! Dang you! That hurt!"

"Hey, look what I got." I handed John Clayton a little piece of birdshot. "Here, wipe your neck. It's just barely bleedin'."

Then we checked our legs and back, and when I looked down at my left leg, right above my ankle, I could see two places that were bleeding. The shot must have hit my bare ankle when I was running down the road. The birdshot was just under the skin, and with a little squeezing they both came out. We had a bunch of other red spots on our back, but the one on John Clayton's neck and the two above my ankle were the only ones to break the skin.

Wow, was John Clayton hot. "Dang you, Richard, you almost got us killed! What if that first blast had hit us? We'd be dead as a Christmas turkey, and I can just hear the preacher at our funeral saying 'These boys were killed stealin' a Christmas tree.' Shoot, we'd go straight to hell so fast, it'd make your head swim."

"Yeah, but he missed with that first shot; thank goodness. Anyway, we ain't hurt much and got a good Christmas tree."

Momma stuck her head in the door. "Boys, that's a beautiful Christmas tree. Where'd y'all get it?"

John Clayton looked at me and waited for me to say something, and I stuttered for a few seconds. "Uh, well, Momma, we were way over near Hugh Burns's little cabin, and we crossed through the big field behind his house. We'd been lookin' for 'bout two hours when I looked over in the edge of the field, and there it was, the perfect Christmas tree."

"Well, I hate that y'all went to so much trouble, but it's a wonderful tree. The best we've ever had."

"Momma, it wasn't much trouble. We just cut it down and carried it home."

Momma smiled and walked back in the kitchen, and John Clayton looked at me, shaking his head.

"You big liar," he hissed. "I can't believe you'd tell all those lies."

Course stealing a Christmas tree and lying to Momma did bother me some, and I tried to come up with something that didn't make it sound so bad.

"Listen, John Clayton, I read somewhere in the Bible, I think it was in First Hezekiah, that said 'A lie for a lie and a tooth for a tooth.'"

"What? Wait a minute; that ain't the way it goes. It's somethin' 'bout eyes and teeth."

"Naw, it ain't 'bout eyes; it's lies and I think it means one lie cancels out another; like if you tell two lies at the same time, you're even. It's like you were tellin' the truth. Heck, in science class they even teach that."

"Oh, my God! Baloney! Baloney! Try tellin' that to Brother Taylor. That's a bald-faced lie, and you know it. If you keep lyin' like that, you're gonna go straight to hell!"

Well, John Clayton whined and complained for a while, and then we started going back over the whole thing. Heck, after John Clayton retold how old man Odom spit tobacco juice on his leg, we started laughing and couldn't stop.

"Hey, a watermelon last summer and now a Christmas tree; shoot, old man Odom's gonna have a conniption fit," I said as I rolled on the bed laughing.

John Clayton headed for his house, and I went in to eat supper.

That night I was lying in my bed thinking about the perfect Christmas tree, when I thought about going to Sunday School next Sunday after stealing a Christmas tree and lying to Momma. Well, it bothered me a whole bunch, but not enough to confess—or take the tree back.

17

Christmas Money on the Highway

Friday, December 22nd, 1944

Boy, I sure didn't want to get out of bed that next morning. We were out of school for Christmas and all the other kids were getting to sleep late, but I had to deliver them sorry papers. *Three days 'til Christmas,* I thought. I figured that by Christmas Eve, when me and Daddy did our shopping I'd be lucky to have five dollars.

Later that day I counted my paper route money, and it came to about four dollars. Shoot, I had to buy presents for Momma, Daddy, John Clayton, and Uncle Hugh. I could tell my presents were gonna be kinda small this year. Then it hit me: *Oh, my gosh,* I thought, *what about Rosalie?* A couple of weeks before I'd been in El Dorado and had checked on the price of the red scarf, and the sales lady told me it was on sale for ten dollars. I'd already tried to borrow the ten dollars from Doc, telling him I'd pay him back from my paper route, but Doc said he had a hard and fast rule— no credit for nobody, and that included me. After I begged Daddy for the ten dollars and he turned me down, telling me my paper route money was supposed to be for Christmas presents, I decided the only possible thing I had left was to try the rabbit trap again.

That afternoon I took the rabbit trap back to the end of our garden where I'd seen dozens of rabbits, but after four rats in a row, I knew I had to set the trap a long way from the barn and chicken house. *Dang rats,* I thought. *Shoot, I'll take that trap way down in Flat Creek Swamp. There ain't no rats there.* But you know

I didn't really think I was gonna catch anything. I'd about given up, but, *Heck*, I thought, *maybe I'll get lucky*.

I hauled the rabbit trap down to Flat Creek Swamp in my wagon and set it on the edge of the creek beside the bridge. I'd seen a bunch of rabbits around the base of the bridge almost every time I went fishing last summer. *Shoot, it's now or never*, I thought.

The next morning I ran down to the creek to check the trap only to find all the corn gone and the sliding door still open.

"Dang, how did a rabbit eat all the corn and not trigger the trap?" I muttered. I reset it and put extra corn out and started back home. I'd walked about fifty yards when I felt a bunch more corn in my back pocket, so I walked back to add this corn to the trap. As I got back close to the trap, I figured out why my corn was missing and the trap wasn't tripped. Birds were everywhere pecking up the corn, and a little bird could just walk right by the tripping stick and eat all the corn without tripping the trap. I was so sad as I stood there and watched the birds peck up the corn, but heck, I went ahead and threw all the corn I had left in the back of the trap and headed home.

Tomorrow was Christmas Eve, and me and Daddy were going into town Christmas shopping. Daddy never shopped until Christmas Eve. He said everybody had things on sale. Course Momma wouldn't go cause she said everything was so picked over, so it was always me and Daddy doing our shopping Christmas Eve afternoon. Heck, I hated to even go, since I was gonna hafta buy five Christmas presents with only a little over four dollars. Boy, I could see just little dinky presents, or maybe just a Christmas card.

Sunday, December 24th, 1944

I finished my paper route and farm chores by seven o'clock that morning and ran down to check the rabbit trap. It was my last hope for any Christmas money.

It was just sitting there with the trap door open, empty as all get out. "Heck, nothin' again!" I muttered. "Oh, well, I better head back and get ready for our Christmas shoppin' trip to El Dorado."

I climbed up the steep bank to the highway and started walking back home when out of the corner of my eye I noticed something furry over on the shoulder of the highway. I thought it was a possum or a rabbit that had been run over by a car, but no it wasn't. I turned it over with my boot and looked down at a big mink.

"Oh, my gosh! A mink! Oh my gosh!" Then I was so excited I yelled out as loud as I could, "A mink! A mink! I've found a mink!" I felt just like I was grabbing up a handful of money when I reached down and picked up that mink.

This was unbelievable. I knew Mr. Benton would buy the mink skin if it wasn't damaged. I checked it over carefully, and it seemed to be in good shape. It looked like a car tire had crushed its skull. Soon the mink was in my coat pocket, and I was heading for home, running as fast as I could. I called John Clayton and told him about finding the mink.

"Heck, Richard, whatever you do, don't try to skin it. My uncle killed a big mink, skinned it, and took it over to Mr. Benton's, but Uncle Jim cut the fur all wrong and he got only five dollars for the hide."

"Okay, I won't touch it. Meet me over at Mr. Benton's house, and we'll let him skin it before we go to El Dorado Christmas shoppin'." I was out of the house in seconds, running down the highway heading for Norphlet.

It took me less than fifteen minutes to get to Mr. Benton's. I walked up to his front porch and called out to him just about the time John Clayton ran up. In a few minutes Mr. Benton walked out of the house carrying a cup of coffee.

"Mr. Benton, look what I got!" I said as I held up the mink.

"Well, looks like you got a nice mink there." Mr. Benton took the mink and examined it. "Well, boys, this is a big female mink. You get a better price for a female. Come on 'round back, and let's skin it."

We went around back with Mr. Benton, and in just a few minutes he'd skinned the mink and put the skin on a stretching board.

"Now, let's see how much I owe you." He pulled out a tape measure and measured the length of the skin.

"Hey, this is one big mink. Seventeen inches, and at a dollar an inch that's seventeen dollars I owe you."

Mr. Benton pulled out his billfold and counted out the seventeen dollars while me and John Clayton stood there with our mouths open. Heck, I'd thought I might get as much as ten, but in a million years I never dreamed that mink would bring seventeen.

I thanked Mr. Benton and stuffed the seventeen dollars in my pocket, and we headed back to my house, with me running along skipping, I was so happy.

"Dang it, Richard, you are so lucky. Goin' down to check on that stupid rabbit trap and findin' a seventeen-dollar mink. I can't believe it."

"Shoot, I've got way over twenty dollars now. This is more money than I've ever had in my whole danged entire life, and I'm gonna do some serious Christmas shoppin' this afternoon."

Then I smiled as I thought about giving Rosalie that red scarf. *I'll bet I get a hug,* I thought.

"Hey, you've got that stupid smile on your face again. Must be thinkin' 'bout Rosalie."

I stuttered and mumbled something and took off running as I yelled back at him, "We better run; Daddy's probably waitin' on us."

Daddy was standing out front when we got to the house.

"Boys, y'all almost got left. We need to get on into town. Some of the stores close early on Christmas Eve. Your mother fixed some sandwiches, so get in the car and let's go."

We roared off to El Dorado in our old 1936 Chevy, and in less than thirty minutes Daddy had parked at the 4-6 Service Center. He figured he could get his oil changed and park free. Heck, as many people as there were downtown on Christmas Eve, he could've never found a parking place.

"Boys, be here at three o'clock, and don't be late."

"Yes, sir," we both said as we sprinted out of the garage.

"Come on, John Clayton, I know 'xactly what I'm gonna buy

Rosalie." We ran up to Samples Department Store, and I went straight to the ladies' department and sure enough there was the red scarf. I could hardly catch my breath as I stood there. My hands were shaking and my knees were trembling.

"Uh, miss, I'd like to buy that red scarf."

"Well, young man, you sure have good taste. It's pure cashmere." She held up the scarf, and I rubbed my hand over it. Gosh, it was so soft.

"Uh, what's cashmere?"

"It's special wool. That's why it's so expensive."

"How much is it?"

"Well, it's on our Christmas Eve sale. It's regularly fifteen dollars, but you can have it for ten."

"Ten dollars? You're kidding," hooted John Clayton as he started to walk away.

"Okay, I'll take it."

"What? Richard, that's almost half of your whole Christmas present money."

"I don't care," I whispered. "I've always wanted Rosalie as my girlfriend, and I'm gonna buy her that red scarf." Heck, I knew I could stretch the other ten dollars I had left to buy the other presents.

Well, I bought the red scarf, and then I went over to where the ladies' clothes were, and I bought Momma some gloves with rabbit fur on the insides. Momma loves anything with fur on it. I bought Daddy a cigarette lighter and a little later I bought John Clayton a knife. Christmas shopping was about over for me. I counted the money I had left, and I had a little less than four dollars.

John Clayton had separated earlier to buy me something, and we met back up in front of Woolworth's. We were going over our presents to be sure we hadn't missed anybody.

"Hey, wait a minute Richard. We forgot 'bout Uncle Hugh."

"Yeah, you're right. How 'bout if I buy 'em a new corncob pipe, and you can buy 'em a pouch of tobacco?"

"Okay, let's go get it."

In a few minutes we walked out of Hall's Drug Store with Uncle Hugh's pipe and tobacco in a little brown paper bag.

"Well, how much money do you have left?" I said to John Clayton.

"Oh, maybe a couple of dollars. How much do you have?"

A little over three dollars."

"Heck, we need to get this wrapped up. We can't give this to Uncle Hugh in this ugly sack."

"Oh, I don't know, Richard. Uncle Hugh probably can't tell the difference in a brown paper bag and a Christmas wrappin'."

"Uuh?"

"Well, he can barely see. It won't do no good to wrap his present."

"Oh, my gosh!" The thought of Uncle Hugh sitting in that little cabin not being able to read the Bible flashed across my mind.

18

Rethinking the Christmas Presents

Sunday, December 24th, 1944

I thought about Rosalie, Momma, Daddy, and Uncle Hugh. Then I pulled the red scarf out of the sack and imagined giving it to Rosalie. *Rosalie will be so happy to get this scarf,* I thought. *Yes, she's a great girl, and she deserves this scarf. Heck, I've been tryin' for a whole month to earn enough money to buy the scarf.* I'd made up my mind. I put the red scarf back in the sack and headed for the 4-6 Service Center to go home, but before I'd gone fifty yards, I had second thoughts.

Every step I took seemed to be an effort as I slowly walked toward the garage. We rounded the corner and I could see the garage in the next block, and it looked like Daddy was already there standing by the car waiting for us. John Clayton ran ahead of me, and he was waving for me to come on, but I couldn't get Uncle Hugh off my mind. I could see him sitting in front of the fireplace in his rocking chair; just sitting; just sitting. I couldn't stand it.

Shoot, that stopped me dead in my tracks, and I yelled at John Clayton, "John Clayton, come here! We ain't through Christmas shoppin' yet!" I turned back and headed for Samples Department Store at a run, and soon we were standing back at the counter where I'd bought the red scarf.

My hands were shaking as I pulled the red scarf out of the sack. It was all I could do to hand it to the sales lady. If I'd been by myself I probably would've cried.

"Ma'am, I changed my mind"—and then I stood there not wanting to turn loose of the red scarf. Shoot, I'd thought of nothing else for a whole month but getting Rosalie that red scarf, and now I had it—but I couldn't make myself keep it. Finally, I said, "I'd like to return this red scarf."

In a few minutes I'd returned Rosalie's red scarf and had the ten dollars back.

My shoulders dropped as I walked out of the store, and I looked over at John Clayton and said, "Let's go, John Clayton; between the two of us, we've got the fifteen dollars now, and we're gonna buy Uncle Hugh those readin' glasses."

"That's great, Richard. Anyway, Rosalie weren't expectin' no present from you, and Valentine's is comin' up in February. You can get her the red scarf then."

"Yeah, I know she's not expectin' me to get her nothin', but you know, the best presents are the ones you don't expect. Shoot, by Valentine's Day it'll probably be so warm she won't need a scarf." I was depressed, but I thought, *At least we'll get Uncle Hugh some reading glasses, and he won't hafta sit there in his rockin' chair doing nothin'.*

I looked back across the street at Samples Department Store just as the last customer left, and a man locked the door. The lights went out and my hopes to get the red scarf vanished. *Dang, so much for the red scarf,* I thought, but more bad news was coming up.

We walked over to Washington Street to the eye doctor's office, but as I got closer to the office I didn't see any lights on inside. My gosh, did I have a bad feeling as we walked up to the door.

Please God, don't let it be closed, I silently prayed. But it was. "Oh, no! It's closed!" I yelled. The sign on the door said, CLOSED EARLY FOR CHRISTMAS EVE. My shoulders slumped, and I felt as low as I've ever felt.

"What are we gonna do now?" We walked over to the front of the store and sat down on the curb. I was almost in tears. My gosh, I was so sad. The eye doctor's office was closed, and so was Samples. No red scarf and no eyeglasses for Uncle Hugh. Things were about as bad as they could be.

"Shoot, maybe someone's still in there. I'm gonna go shake the door," said John Clayton as he got up and walked over to the door.

"Forget it, John Clayton. It's Christmas Eve, and everybody's done gone home. Let's head back to the garage to meet Daddy."

John Clayton was shaking the door and yelling through the keyhole when this man walked up.

"Hey! Young man! What are you doing?"

I looked up, and it was the eye doctor. My hopes soared. "Oh, sir, you're just the person we're lookin' for."

"Aren't you the boys who took the eye chart home to check out a friend?"

"Yes, sir, but we didn't have the money to pay for the glasses. We've got the money now. Will you let us in and sell us the glasses?"

"Well, boys, I quit a little early today, and I've been down at the Olympic for a few beers, but, why not? After all it's Christmas Eve."

The doctor opened the office, turned on the lights, and soon he'd found Uncle Hugh's new glasses.

"Here they are, boys. By the way, who's your friend that needs these glasses?"

"His name is Hugh Burns, sir, and he hasn't been able to read the Bible for a whole year. He lives in a little cabin back in the woods and gets by on a railroad pension of fifty-five dollars a month. He's 'bout a hunnerd years old, and he's one of our best friends," said John Clayton.

"You mean, y'all have gone to all this trouble and have come up with this money to help an old colored man?"

"Yes, sir, but you don't know Uncle Hugh; if you did, you'd know why we wanted these glasses. He's a wonderful man, and he tells the best stories. Thank you so much for openin' your store. Here's the fifteen dollars." I handed the eye doctor the money, and he looked at us for a few seconds; not saying a word.

Then he said, "Uh, well, boys, it sounds like Uncle Hugh is a pretty good man, and he sure has two good friends in you two. Here, take this five dollars back and buy something good to eat for Uncle Hugh's Christmas dinner; maybe a big turkey."

"Wow, thank you sir. We sure will," I said.

Me and John Clayton left the office and hurried down to the 4-6 Service Center where Daddy was waiting for us.

"Boys, y'all are late again. Just foolin' 'round and forgot the time, huh?"

"Yes, sir, I'm sorry," I said.

"Well, hop in, and let's go home. I've got to pick up a few Christmas things from Alley's Grocery before we leave town."

Daddy loves Alley's. It's not a big grocery store, but it has some food already cooked up and ready to eat. I whispered in John Clayton's ear, "We can spend the five dollars in Alley's. They got a lot of really good stuff, maybe even a roast turkey."

John Clayton nodded as Daddy pulled up, and we all went in. Daddy went one way, and me and John Clayton went straight back to where the cooked foods were. There on the top of the counter was a big roast turkey.

"Sir; how much is that turkey?"

"Son, it's been sold, and that's the last one," said the man behind the counter.

"Do you have anything else that could be served for Christmas dinner?"

"Naw, we sold out everything we had. Oh, wait a minute, someone sent this goose back. Said their wife didn't like goose. It's a twelve-fifty goose, but I'll let you have it for eight and a half."

"We ain't got but five dollars, and we're buyin' it for an old man that's not gonna have any Christmas dinner if we don't bring him somethin'," I said.

"Is that the truth, boys?"

"Yes, sir, we promise."

The man looked at us for a few seconds, and then slowly nodded his head. "Well, okay, let me mark this ticket."

"Sir, could you put it in one of them Christmas sacks. It's a surprise present," John Clayton said.

"Dang, boy, I've already given you a heck of a deal. Those sacks are a dollar each. Oh, well, it's Christmas Eve, I guess so."

He put the goose in the Christmas sack. We checked out and started for the car. Daddy walked out with a sack of Christmas-type food, and we headed home.

We pulled up in our driveway, and me and John Clayton jumped out.

"Daddy, we've got some presents to deliver. I'll be back after-while."

"Okay, be home by dark."

"Yes, sir."

19

Christmas Eve
with Uncle Hugh

Sunday, December 24th, 1944

Wow, I was excited about giving Uncle Hugh his glasses, and I'd just about put Rosalie out of my mind. *Heck*, I thought, *Rosalie really didn't need that red scarf.* Course I'm always trying to make things okay by saying stuff I really don't mean. Yeah, it did bother me a bunch, but then I thought about old Uncle Hugh not being able to read the Bible. *Shoot, he needs these glasses a whole lot more than Rosalie needs that red scarf.* I almost had myself convinced.

It was about four o'clock when we left my house heading for Uncle Hugh's little cabin. Early that morning a cold front had whistled into south Arkansas, and it had gotten colder all day long. By late afternoon the temperature was down to below thirty degrees and a strong wind was blowing right out of the north. Dang, it was cold! As we trudged along we pulled our jackets tightly around our necks trying to keep the bitter, cutting north wind, which was whipping around us, from chilling us to the bone. That didn't work worth a flip, and we walked along toward Uncle Hugh's freezing to death.

"Look at those clouds, John Clayton." I pointed to a cloud bank in the west. "They look like snow clouds to me."

"Ha, fat chance of snow 'round here. A couple of days ago I asked my daddy if he remembered it ever snowin' on Christmas, and he told me that in forty-five years he ain't never seen it snow even during the entire Christmas week. You're dreamin' if you think it's gonna snow tonight."

"Yeah, you're probably right, but wouldn't it be something if it did?"

John Clayton nodded, and we plodded along until we reached the lane leading to Uncle Hugh's cabin.

We could see the smoke from his fireplace, and his coal oil lantern was glowing in the window. We walked along carrying the sack with the roast goose and the little case with his glasses, shaking we were so cold.

"Dang, John Clayton, I'm freezin', let's get inside by Uncle Hugh's fireplace.

Uncle Hugh! Uncle Hugh! It's John Clayton and Richard!"

In a few seconds Uncle Hugh opened the door and came out to the edge of his front porch. He was smiling the biggest smile you ever did see.

"Boys, what y'all up too? It's Christmas Eve, ain't there a bunch of stuff goin' on 'round your house?"

"Well, Uncle Hugh, Momma waits 'til it's good and dark before she starts our Christmas Eve stuff. We've got plenty of time to come see you, and we've got you two surprise presents." I held up the glasses, and John Clayton held up the roast goose.

"Sho nuf?"

"Heck, Uncle Hugh, it's Christmas," said John Clayton, "and you don't think we'd forget you; do you?"

Uncle Hugh gave us another big smile and waved us in.

"Come on in, boys, 'fore we all freezes to death. Y'all is mighty good friends to come out in weather like this, just to bring me a Christmas present."

"You bet, Uncle Hugh; let me get by that fire," John Clayton said as he sprinted up the steps and through the door.

When I walked into Uncle Hugh's cabin I noticed something; he'd decorated for Christmas. It was such a surprise that I just stopped there right inside the door and looked.

"Gosh, Uncle Hugh, you've decorated for Christmas." Sure enough, Uncle Hugh had a little cedar tree, some holly hanging from his fireplace, and he had even strung some holly berries and popcorn on some twine and had hung them on the little cedar tree. There was nothing under the tree except two little brown sacks tied with green ribbon. In the soft glow of the coal oil lantern the Christmas decorations just seemed just perfect.

"This is really great, Uncle Hugh," said John Clayton.

Me and John Clayton got over in front of the fireplace turning back and forth like some chicken on a spit trying to warm up, and Uncle Hugh sat down and leaned back in his rocking chair right beside the fireplace. We stood there in the dim light from the coal oil lantern warming by the fireplace, listening to the wind rattle the tin roof and windows, as Uncle Hugh went over to his old woodstove and fixed us a cup of hot chocolate.

"Boys, I done saved this coco for a special time, and I guess it don't get no more special than this." He handed us a cup of hot chocolate, and we backed up to the fireplace as we sipped it.

"Gosh, this hot chocolate tastes great, especially on a cold day like this," John Clayton said.

I could hardly wait for Uncle Hugh to try out his new glasses, so I poked John Clayton and motioned for him to give Uncle Hugh the glasses.

John Clayton pulled out Uncle Hugh's new glasses.

"Uncle Hugh, guess what we have right here in this little case." John Clayton held the small black case over his head and waved it back and forth.

"Well, I don't have no idea."

"It's some new readin' glasses; your Christmas present from me and Richard. Here, Uncle Hugh, see if they work."

Uncle Hugh couldn't believe it. He opened the case, looked the glasses over, and finally put them on.

"Oh, boys, I thinks they's too strong. I can't hardly see y'all."

"Shoot, Uncle Hugh, those glasses are for readin' and seein' close stuff. Go get the Bible and see if you can read it," I said.

Uncle Hugh took off his glasses, walked over to the mantle, and picked up his old Bible. He sat down in his rocking chair, put on his new glasses, and slowly opened the Bible.

"Go on, Uncle Hugh; read something. We wanta know if they work," said John Clayton.

"Boys, it's Christmas Eve, and you just don't read jus' any part of the Bible on Christmas Eve. I'm gonna turn to the Christmas story in the book of Luke."

In a minute he'd found the place where he wanted to start, and he started to read: *"In those days Caesar Augustus decreed that all the world..."* Uncle Hugh stopped; there was a long pause and as I looked at him I could see his lips starting to tremble and tears began to fill his eyes. Uncle Hugh dropped his head and sat there quietly for a couple of minutes while we stood by the fire and watched him. Finally, he raised his head and smiled one of his big smiles with all those white teeth, and he almost shouted; "Oh! Oh! Oh! I can read the Bible again! I can! I can! I can read it!"

Uncle Hugh kept on saying that over and over again as he wiped the tears from his face. I'd been so excited about Uncle Hugh's new glasses that I was laughing and kidding, having a great time. Heck, I'd even forgot about not getting that red scarf for Rosalie—well, almost, but right then I was durn sure glad I'd taken it back and bought Uncle Hugh the glasses. Now, I started to get all choked up as Uncle Hugh went on and on. Maybe I'd have made it if I hadn't looked over at John Clayton as a tear ran down his cheek. That was it. We both started crying, ran over to Uncle Hugh, he put his arms around us, and we all had a great big cry. You know, sometimes, even if you're eleven years old and you know you're too big to cry, it's okay to cry. That was one of them times.

Finally, Uncle Hugh calmed down, and told us to sit down by the fireplace while he read the rest of the Christmas story. After he finished the Christmas story, I picked up the sack with the roast goose in it.

"Uncle Hugh, we've still got another Christmas present. The man that fixed your glasses cut some money off the price and told us to buy a turkey or somethin' for your Christmas dinner with the five dollars he cut off the price."

"Here, Uncle Hugh, open it," John Clayton said.

Uncle Hugh slowly opened the sack and pulled out the big roast goose. "Oh, my Lord; I ain't never had such a Christmas. You boys done outdone yourselves."

Uncle Hugh started to sniff again, and John Clayton said, "Dang it, Uncle Hugh, don't start cryin' again. I can't stand it."

Uncle Hugh smiled, walked over to us, and gave us another big hug, and then set his roasted goose down on the stove.

The old shutters on the window slammed with a bang, the tin roof rattled, and I glanced out the window. "Dang, John Clayton, it's almost dark. Uncle Hugh, we gotta go. I told Daddy I'd be home by dark."

"Okay, boys, but first let me get y'all's Christmas presents." Uncle Hugh walked over to the little Christmas tree and picked up the two little sacks tied with green ribbon. "Here you go, boys, open 'um up."

We opened the presents. In each sack was a carved whistle, and according to Uncle Hugh, they weren't just whistles, they were cane flutes with holes, and you could learn to play songs on them.

"Boys, I done carved them all by myself. Now, y'all needs to learn how to play 'um, cause when I'm gone y'all can remember me every time you blows them whistles."

"Oh, Uncle Hugh, don't talk like that. It's Christmas and we're gonna spend a lot more Christmases with you," I said.

Uncle Hugh didn't say nothing, but out of the corner of my eye, I could see him slowly shake his head. *I wonder why he did that,* I thought.

"Gosh, Uncle Hugh, these are great," I said as I blew my whistle.

"Heck, Richard, we can use these whistles to keep in touch when we're down in Flat Creek Swamp," John Clayton said.

We sat down by the fire, and Uncle Hugh put another couple of pieces of wood in the fireplace, which really made for a great fire.

"Wow, does that fire feel good!" John Clayton said. "Richard, I think we can stay another thirty minutes and still make it home by dark. For some reason I don't want to go anywheres right now."

He leaned back against the side of Uncle Hugh's rocking chair and started to blow on his whistle.

I nodded, and Uncle Hugh smiled. "Boys, hand me one of them flutes, and I'll show y'all how to play it."

Well, Uncle Hugh could sure play that flute, and for the next ten minutes he played everything from "Yankee Doodle" to "My Old Kentucky Home."

We sat there around the fire with Uncle Hugh playing old songs, some I'd never heard of, then he said, "Well, it's Christmas, I guess I should play some Christmas carols," and he started to play "Silent Night." About halfway through he stopped and looked over at us. "Boys, y'all sing 'long while I play."

"Uncle Hugh, I can't sing a lick, but John Clayton is always in all the singin' stuff at church. He's a real good singer."

"Aw, Richard, I just can't sing sittin' here while Uncle Hugh plays his whistle."

"Shore you can, John Clayton. Just stand up right here beside me where you can hear this flute, and when I nods my head you start a-singin'."

Well, I had to give John Clayton a push, but he finally stood up. Uncle Hugh started playing, and then he nodded his head at John Clayton.

"Silent Night, Holy night, all is calm, all is bright...."

A cold wind whistled through the trees, shook the old tin roof, and rattled the shutters on the cabin as we huddled closer to the fire. John Clayton sang through the first verse of "Silent Night," and Uncle Hugh just went on and on about how good a singer John Clayton was. Course that was enough to get John Clayton to sing a verse of "Away in a Manger."

As we sat and talked with Uncle Hugh, he told us stories of Christmases when he was a little boy and how his momma would always make him a special red Christmas cap that, according to Uncle Hugh, made him the envy of every kid at school.

I took another look at Uncle Hugh's Christmas decorations, and in the light of the fire the holly berries sparkled and his little cedar tree seemed just right for the little cabin. As we sat there Uncle Hugh played a bunch more Christmas carols and John Clayton started singing again.

Wow, this really is Christmas, I thought. You know, sometimes things are so good that you just want them to stay that way and never change, but they don't. I took another look out the window, and I could barely see the big oak tree in Uncle Hugh's front yard. It was almost dark.

I really didn't want to go, but I knew we had to.

"Uncle Hugh, we really gotta go."

"Boys, y'all wait just a minute. I done got y'all a special present, and it ain't no Christmas present. Come on over here. I wants us to have a good talk." I started to move closer to Uncle Hugh, looking up at his smiling face, when suddenly he looked as if he was in pain. His head tilted, and one hand crossed over and pressed against his chest.

"Oh, oh, oh," he mumbled, and he slumped back in his rocking chair.

"Uncle Hugh, what's wrong? What's wrong?" It scared me to death, and I grabbed his hand.

He took a deep breath and relaxed, shaking his head as if nothing was wrong. "Ain't much of nothin', Richard, I just gets a sharp pain sometimes. It'll go away in a few minutes."

Uncle Hugh tried to keep talking, but he was breathing little shallow breaths, and he could hardly get a word out. Finally, he said, "Boys, I guess I'm just gettin' old—I'm alright now—I got something here I want y'all to have." He reached in his pocket and pulled out his railroad watch. We both knew how proud Uncle Hugh was of that watch. Heck, it was the only thing Uncle Hugh owned worth anything. He'd sit around during the day and polish it until it shined like a new penny.

"Y'all see this railroad watch?"

"Yes, sir," we both said.

"Well, I want y'all to have it."

"Oh, no, Uncle Hugh, we're not 'bout to take your railroad

watch," I said.

"Yeah, Uncle Hugh, you'd just be lost if you didn't have that watch," said John Clayton.

"Boys, let me tell you somethin'. These glasses, the pipe and tobacco, and the Christmas goose is real nice, and I appreciates it so much, but that ain't why I'm a-givin' you this watch."

Heck, we didn't have a clue what Uncle Hugh was talking about. We looked at Uncle Hugh with a puzzled look as he continued.

"You see, boys, one of these days—and—uh, well, I don't know how to tell y'all this." Uncle Hugh stopped for a few seconds, then he said, "Real soon I'm gonna go to be with Jesus, and I knows it ain't long. I's got a bad hurtin' in my chest, and sometimes I can't even walk to the spring and back without sittin' down. Oh, I know what's wrong, my old heart's 'bout to go. Ain't gonna be long 'til somebody knocks on my door, and when I don't answer, they's gonna walk in and I'll just be lyin' on my old bed, done passed. Boys—this'll be my last Christmas with y'all."

"Oh, Uncle Hugh, don't talk like that. Let me get Daddy to take you into El Dorado and see a doctor."

"Richard, I'm done ready to pass, and I don't wanta see no doctor. I's gonna sit here, read my Bible, and wait for Jesus to come take me home. He's done gettin' them angels ready to come get me."

"Uncle Hugh, we're gonna have a bunch more Christmases with you. I don't want to here 'nother word 'bout you not being here next Christmas. You're 'bout to make me cry again," said John Clayton.

"Now, come on, y'all, don't tune up and cry. This is one of the happiest days of my life. Y'all is my bestest friends, and I wants y'all to have this watch, cause when I passes, somebody's gonna get that watch, and it ain't gonna be the folks I want to have it. Here, Richard, take it. You keep it a week, and then John Clayton can keep it a week."

Uncle Hugh put the railroad watch in my hand and slowed closed my fingers around it, and then I felt his hand tighten around mine. He had that look again.

"Uncle Hugh, what is it? Is it hurtin' again?" He nodded and slipped back in the rocking chair and held his chest for at least a couple of minutes. As he started to take some deep breaths again he started talking to us in a real soft voice. "Boys,—for the last few days—the pain been a-gettin' worse and worse and—today it's comin' most of the time. Ain't gonna be long now."

"Uncle Hugh, let me go get Daddy, and he'll take you to the doctor in El Dorado," I begged.

"Richard, I appreciates you wantin' to do that, but I done made my peace."

Uncle Hugh had tears in his eyes now as he said, "Before y'all go, I just wanta say goodbye one more time. Come here, Richard, you're such a good friend."

I moved over right by the rocking chair, and Uncle Hugh put his arms around me and held me close for a long time. "Goodbye, Richard; and John Clayton, come here." He put his big rough hands around John Clayton's shoulders and pulled him against his chest. "Goodbye, John Clayton, and just remember the good times we had. Boys, y'all done come to see me twice a week for the past year and bought me my groceries. Every time y'all come by here it just made my day. I'd just sit at the window lookin' and waitin' for y'all to come see me."

"Heck, Uncle Hugh, weren't you lonesome and bored?" I said.

"Naw, boys, when you've had a life as good as mine you can just sit on the front porch and think back over all the good times and good friends. Some days I'd sit on the porch and think back on that first day of work for the railroad. Sometimes I'd think 'bout when y'all was lost and walked up to my cabin. Oh, I've had a good life, and now I'm just old and wore out. Just like an old car that ready for the dump. Now, don't y'all worry none 'bout me. I'm on my way to the Promised Land."

"Don't say that, Uncle Hugh!"

"Yeah, Uncle Hugh," said John Clayton, "that hurtin' will probably pass."

Uncle Hugh smiled and leaned back in his rocking chair.

"Richard, before you go turn up the wick on that coal oil lantern on the table."

"Sure, Uncle Hugh." I walked over and turned up the wick, and the room glowed in the soft light of the lantern. John Clayton looked out the window again to see if it was getting dark.

"Heck, Richard, it's almost dark, we gotta go; come on."

I started for the door as Uncle Hugh looked up from his rocking chair.

"Just a minute, Richard; I got somethin' else." Uncle Hugh reached in his pocket and pulled out a letter.

"Richard, y'all keep this letter in case somebody thinks y'all stole this watch. It says I gave it to you, and I signed my name right at the bottom."

I looked at John Clayton, and he looked at me. We couldn't help it; we broke down and started crying again.

"Boys, stop that cryin'. Listen to me. Y'all has given me the bestest Christmas that anybody could ever have, and I don't want no sad faces when you leave here. Listen, if you want to make me happy, just enjoy this Christmas and have fun, no matter what happens. Do y'all hear me? No matter what happens." Uncle Hugh paused and then said it again, "Now, no matter what happens. Y'all understand?" We looked at Uncle Hugh and then at each other for several minutes, then through misty eyes, I said; "Yes, sir."

I bit my lip to keep from crying as Uncle Hugh waved us out the door. "Y'all better hurry on home. It's gittin' dark. Y'all just throw some snowballs at each other and forget about me. You hear?"

"Heck, Uncle Hugh, it not snowin' and you know it never snows 'round here on Christmas," said John Clayton.

He smiled and softly said, "Just you wait, boys. You'll see."

"Well, Merry Christmas, Uncle Hugh. We gotta go before this cold north wind freezes my skinny neck," I said.

Uncle Hugh smiled, acted like he remembered something, and then said, "Richard, wait just a minute. I got somethin' else for you, maybe you can use it. I shore ain't gonna have no need for it."

"What?" We walked back up on the porch and stood there waiting for Uncle Hugh.

"The ladies from the church done brought me a Christmas basket with some cookies, and they put some other stuff in there that I ain't never gonna use."

20

The Red Scarf

Sunday, December 24th, 1944

It wasn't but a couple of minutes until Uncle Hugh came back out on the porch with something wrapped up in a piece of white tissue paper.

"Here you go, Richard. Maybe this'll keep that north wind from freezin' you."

Uncle Hugh handed me the little package, and I pulled the tissue paper off. For at least a whole minute I couldn't say a word—It was a red scarf.

"Oh, my gosh! Oh, my gosh! A red scarf!" I finally managed to mumble. "Thank you! Thank you! Uncle Hugh."

"Well, Richard; that ain't no big gift, cause it's just somethin' I'd never use, and I thought you'd like it. I don't believe I've ever seen no one that excited over just a red scarf."

My mind was twirling as I grabbed Uncle Hugh and gave him a great big hug. "A red scarf! A red scarf!" It just kept flooding through my mind. I put the red scarf in my jacket pocket and looked over at John Clayton, who was shaking his head.

"Dang, findin' a mink on the highway, and then getting' a red scarf for Rosalie just handed to you. I don't believe it!"

I smiled and did a little jig on the porch, and we were just about to leave when Uncle Hugh reached over and grabbed the door facing to keep from falling.

"Uncle Hugh! What's wrong?" I said. I ran back to where he was standing and braced myself against him to keep him from falling.

"Boys, I done got that pain again, and it's real bad this time. I need y'all to help me get back to my rockin' chair where I can rest 'til it goes away."

John Clayton got on one side of Uncle Hugh and I got on the other side, and he slowly walked back in the cabin to the rocking chair. Finally, he sat down and leaned back, trying to catch his breath.

"Uncle Hugh, please let me go get my daddy. He'll drive you over to El Dorado to see the doctor."

"Richard, I knows you wants to do something, but I ain't goin' to leave this place. Now you boys head on home. I'm gonna just rest in this rockin' chair 'til the angels come to take me away. They'll turn off my old coal oil lantern and take me to heaven."

Well, it was no use talking to Uncle Hugh about leaving. He wasn't about to go anywhere. We said our goodbyes and walked out of the cabin.

We walked down the dirt lane from Uncle Hugh's little cabin, and when we got to the end of the lane where the spring was located we stopped and looked back. The north wind whipped our hair, and we pulled our jackets up around our ears to keep warm. In the late afternoon light we could barely make out a wisp of smoke coming out the chimney and the coal oil lantern light in the window. We didn't say a word for a couple of minutes, and then, just before we turned to leave, I nudged John Clayton. "Look, John Clayton, the lantern just went out." We stood there in the gathering darkness, staring at the little cabin which was dark now, with tears streaming down our cheeks.

"Oh, Uncle Hugh, Uncle Hugh." I sobbed. "He's gone." We stood there a few more minutes, and then we looked at each other.

"Richard, remember what Uncle Hugh said?"

"Yeah, he said that no matter what happened, he wanted us to have a good Christmas."

As I stood there with John Clayton, I opened the tissue paper wrapping again and looked at the red scarf. It was new and still had the tags on it. I smiled and nodded my head.

The wind had shifted out of the north right after lunch, and now the bitter cold air of the arctic cold front that had swept across south Arkansas was reaching its full fury. We pulled our thin jackets tighter around our necks and hurried along in the dim light. Finally, we reached Norphlet just as it got dark. The street-lights came on as we trudged along, heading for home.

"Hey, maybe it'll snow," said John Clayton.

"Shoot, it never snows around here on Christmas," I mumbled, but just as I said that I thought about what Uncle Hugh had said.

Then, as we passed under a streetlight, I looked up and I saw the first flakes of snow start to drift down.

"Snow! John Clayton, it's snowin'!"

"Oh, my gosh! Uncle Hugh—how did he know?"

"Uncle Hugh just knew, John Clayton. He just knew. I don't know how, but he knew."

We came to Hill Kenedy's Grocery, and John Clayton turned and headed for his house.

"Merry Christmas, Richard; see you tomorrow."

"Yeah, Merry Christmas."

Then John Clayton stopped and turned around. We looked at each other for a few seconds and I said, "It was really something; wasn't it?"

"Yeah, I'll never forget tonight."

Then John Clayton headed for his house, and I hurried on toward home. The snow picked up as I walked along through down-town Norphlet, which was closed down tighter than a drum. However, I wasn't going straight home. I had one more present to deliver, and in a few minutes I was standing in front of Rosalie's house. I was so nervous I could hardly stand still. It was dark, and great big snowflakes were slowly drifting down. I looked at the house from the sidewalk and I thought, *Rosalie's whole family is in there, and I'll bet the house is just full of uncles and aunts. Maybe I should wait.* I stood there trying to decide, and then I thought about what Uncle Hugh said, "—just enjoy Christmas and have fun." *Yeah,* I thought. *Uncle Hugh would want me to give this scarf to Rosalie.*

It took a few more minutes for me to get up the courage to walk up the sidewalk and knock on the door. There was a lot of talking inside and no one heard me, and I had to knock again. Finally, the door opened and Mrs. Davis looked out, saw me standing there under the porch light, and said, "Richard?"

"Yes ma'am." And then I froze for what seemed like minutes. Mrs. Davis said, "Yes?"

Finally, I blurted out, "Could I see Rosalie for just a few minutes? I'm sorry to interrupt y'all's Christmas Eve."

Mrs. Davis smiled and reached over and gave me a big hug. "Rosalie! You have a guest."

Mrs. Davis walked back in the house, and I started backing down the steps and stood in the yard, where I could leave quickly in case Rosalie didn't come out. I didn't want to stand there in front of the door under the porch light like some idiot.

"Richard?"

It was Rosalie, who had opened the door and walked out on the porch.

"Yes, I'm out here."

"Why are you standing out in the front yard?"

"Oh, I was just watchin' it snow. Isn't it great?"

"Yeah, it sure is, Richard." She walked down the steps and came over to where I was standing.

I was breathing little short breaths, and even as cold as it was my hands were sweating. We stood there for another minute or so watching the snow fall, and then I finally got up the courage to take the red scarf out of my pocket.

"Rosalie, I have a Christmas present for you." I handed her the red scarf wrapped in tissue paper, as I tried to keep my hands from shaking.

"Oh, Richard, what is it?" she said as she took the paper and began to unwrap it.

"I'm sorry I didn't have it wrapped. I just didn't have time."

"Oh, don't worry 'bout that. Gift wrapping just gets in the way."

Rosalie took the last piece of tissue off and unfolded the red scarf.

"Richard! It's wonderful! You know how much I love red, and I've needed a scarf for a long time. Oh, thank you! Thank you!"

We were standing kinda close and Rosalie was right in front of me. She reached out to give me a little hug, and I thought she was planning to give me a kiss on the cheek. However, I guess, since I'm left-handed, I turned exactly the opposite way, and then instead of a kiss on the cheek our lips met head on. Wow! There was a stunned pause from both of us, and we kept our lips together for a long long time. Well, actually it was only a few seconds.

Then Rosalie said, "Richard, that was my first kiss."

"Mine too." Then I reached down and took her by the hand.

We held hands for a few more minutes until Mrs. Davis came to the door and yelled for Rosalie to come back in. I wanted to kiss her again, but I decided not to push my luck. It had been a wonderful Christmas Eve.

I left Rosalie's house and headed for home, fairly skipping along as I headed down the El Dorado highway toward our house. It was bitter cold, and the wind was blowing so hard the snow was stinging my face. However, I didn't pay any attention to being cold; Rosalie was all that was on my mind, until I reached in my pocket to warm my hands and felt Uncle Hugh's watch. There was a streetlight on the El Dorado highway about a hundred yards from our house, and I stopped under it to take another look at Uncle Hugh's watch. I opened the case and in the dim light I could see an inscription on the back of the case. Something had been scratched out, and below it Uncle Hugh had cut some words. Standing there with a Christmas Eve snow falling on my shoulders in the dim light of the streetlight I read: REMEMBER ME, MY GOOD FRIENDS: HUGH BURNS, DECEMBER 24TH, 1944.

I stood there a long time just thinking about Uncle Hugh, not caring a bit that the falling snow was starting to matt in my hair. The inscription was a little rough since he'd cut it with his pocket knife, but considering his bad eyes, it was a real good job. *He must have planned this a long time ago,* I thought as I stared at the watch. Finally, I closed the watch and put it in my pocket and trudged on down the dark road.

What a Christmas! I'll never ever forget it as long as I live, I thought as I walked down the road toward home, holding my face up to catch the snowflakes. Right before I got home I had the strangest feeling, like I needed to say something. I stopped right in the middle of the road; I smiled, looked up at the sky, and said, "Thanks, Uncle Hugh."

I brushed the snow out of my hair, ran the last fifty yards to my house, and opened the kitchen door with a yell; "It's snowin'! It's snowin'!"

Daddy looked up from the radio, and Momma walked to the kitchen window. "Jack, it really is snowin', great big flakes; and it's stickin'."